NORTH OF THE PORT

Also by Anthony Bukoski
Twelve Below Zero
Children of Strangers
Polonaise
Time Between Trains

STORIES

NORTH OF THE PORT

ANTHONY BUKOSKI

Southern Methodist University Press / Dallas

This collection of stories is a work of fiction. Names, characters, places, and incidents are either the product of the author's imagination or are used fictitiously.

Requests for permission to reproduce material from this work should be sent to:
Rights and Permissions
Southern Methodist University Press
PO Box 750415
Dallas, Texas 75275-0415

A number of the stories in this collection first appeared in other publications: "Gossamer Bloom" was published as "The Light Easterly Breeze" in *Great River Review*; "Report of the Guardian of the Sick" appeared in *War, Literature & the Arts*; "The Shadow Players" originally appeared in *Image*. Reprinted with permission. "The Case for Bread and Sausage" was published as "Mission Work" in *Barnstorm: Contemporary Wisconsin Fiction* (University of Wisconsin Press, 2005). "A Walk Down Lonely Street" appeared as "Love Me Tender" in *New Mexico Humanities Review*; "The Wand of Youth" in *Chronicles: A Magazine of American Culture*; "One Red Rose on a New Black Dress" in *Western Humanities Review*; and "The Wally Na Zdrowie Show" as "A Bowl of Stew" in *Chronicles: A Magazine of American Culture*. The author is grateful to the editors of these magazines and to the University of Wisconsin Press anthology for permission to reprint.

Cover art: *Icebound Lake Boat* by Charles Burchfield. Smithsonian American Art Museum, Gift of the Charles E. Burchfield Foundation

Jacket and text design by Kellye Sanford

Library of Congress Cataloging-in-Publication Data
Bukoski, Anthony.
    North of the port : stories / Anthony Bukoski. — 1st ed.
        p. cm.
    ISBN 978-0-87074-521-8 (alk. paper)
1. Wisconsin—Social life and customs—Fiction. 2. Polish Americans—Fiction. I. Title.

PS3552.U399N67 2008
813'.54—dc22

2007049806

Printed in the United States of America on acid-free paper

10 9 8 7 6 5 4 3 2 1

For John and Gertrude Zabaski

ACKNOWLEDGMENTS

My deepest thanks, always, go to Kathryn Lang, my editor for sixteen years. I am indebted as well to Professor Thomas Napierkowski, University of Colorado–Colorado Springs, for first encouraging me to write about the Polish Americans of northern Wisconsin, my people. For their kindness to me, I thank Barton Sutter and Gordon Weaver, good friends, good writers, and Steven Doherty, fellow East Ender. I am also grateful to Shirley Ann Grau, of Metairie, Louisiana, and to Fraser and Dian Snowden, of Natchitoches, Louisiana, who, long ago, befriended a northerner in love with the South. Finally, my wife Elaine's great patience and generosity of spirit have again enabled me to write a book.

CONTENTS

GOSSAMER BLOOM

On Assumption Day in August 1950, when the Blessed Virgin is taken soul and body into heaven, thousands of threadlike strands began falling from a sky as blue as the Virgin's robes. Old women leaving Mass in the East End of Superior, Wisconsin, cried, "Look up there! Here are Jesus' white hairs. He is unhappy with the world!"

With the sunlight reflecting off of them, the long threads of Assumption Day fell over the coalyard and the ore dock. They caught on the front door of the church, caught against Polish faces, settled softly on the hair and clothes of Polish workmen at the flour mill and the oil dock. Six hours later, Andrzej Iwanowski saw the white strands float down. He'd been to Mass, been to the docks, seen Mrs. Podgorak lifting her hands to feel the strands on her way into the garage where she'd gone to look at herself in the mirror, seen her capturing them with her hands—and still the white strands floated down hour upon hour. He saw them at the railroad switching station on Ninth Street.

In an article in that evening's paper, a biologist from the teachers' college explained that orb-web spiders were hatching their young. The spiderlings climb trees, bushes, and telephone poles to send out silk threads from their abdomens. Long strands on a windless Assumption Day, the weblines sail straight up. Caught by the light winds aloft, the spiderlings on the end of weblines fall to earth. On "gossamer bloom days," the blossoming of orb-web spiders is unusually heavy, wrote the biologist, which is why people noticed them in the East End. No longer clustering together, the spiderlings, after their scattered journeys, are less likely to be preyed on by birds.

Soon after, the professor, in his zeal, sent a special dispatch informing the paper that people from Sheboygan to Milwaukee had once witnessed a similar occurrence when spiderlings rode the winds one hundred miles across Lake Michigan to the eastern shore of Wisconsin. This time the weblines had crossed Lake Superior, the Great Sweetwater Sea, to fall on Superior's East End.

The young man Andrzej Iwanowski and the lovely Magda Podgorak took this bloom seriously—Magda so seriously she tried flying. Felix Podgorak, her husband, took what had happened seriously, too. Wounded in the European theater, he was a veteran home six years now from the war. The best he could figure, when he related his wife's story to his friends, Andrzej's parents, a week later, was that she had accepted the Lord's counsel in the form of the white strands, gone into the garage, looked at her image in a mirror stored there, then headed east to the railroad trestle. What but a sign from Jesus could have possessed a churchgoing woman to gaze heavenward, take a deep breath, and soar outward from the trestle trying to capture weblines? For years it had seemed to St. Adalbert's parishioners—and to Andrzej, a displaced person who'd recently come here from Poland with his family—that bird-like chirps were rising from her chest as she struggled for air in the incense-filled church. Magda Podgorak had asthma, emphysema; perhaps something else was wrong with her, something in her mind. She was always looking for Jesus. In mirrors, she sought His image, and in the autumn sky, in the ice that forms caves along the Sweetwater Sea, in the moonlight that shines into those caves. You'd see her walking in out-of-the-way places thinking Jesus was there. On Assumption Day,

Andrzej thought the gossamer bloom had convinced Mrs. Podgorak that the birds dwelling in her chest would carry and keep her aloft, as would the weblines from heaven. This way she could see Jesus sooner.

Finished at the railroad salvage site where he'd assisted the workers that afternoon, Andrzej, who was nineteen years old, perceptive, and lived nearby, was calculating how much the company would make from its salvage operation. Through most of the afternoon, Mrs. Podgorak was far from his thoughts, though he'd observed her at other times when he did chores for Felix and his wife. At their house one day, Andrzej had seen her tapping her pale lips with pale fingers, asking, "My God, why hast Thou forsaken me?" as she stood before the mirror attached to a wooden dresser they stored in the garage. To keep the dresser in a bedroom of the house would have meant more sorrow when the Podgoraks already had enough mirrors to look into for sorrow, the boy decided as he watched her from his hiding spot.

Leaning forward, Magda Podgorak had touched her lips to the mirror and asked God the question again. The sight of the frail woman, beautiful despite the gray streaking her dark hair, the sight of her kissing herself, kissing the image she believed was God's, troubled Andrzej. No young man should see this. He might think it has to do with sex, something the boy had yet to experience, though he wondered what it was like for Mr. Podgorak to be alone in a bedroom with such a dark, mysterious woman as Magda. Like this wife of his, like Andrzej himself, Mr. Podgorak was also a thinker. Thinking was a bigger problem for her, however, Andrzej concluded after watching her a few times. No doubt the parish women knew how much Mrs. Podgorak's thoughts troubled her. Living in the isolated area of fields and woods between the switching tower and the trestle, with her husband gone at work or at the tavern so much, Magda had time to dwell on the mysteries of Catholic faith in a way that other ladies with their sodalities, bake sales, and children couldn't. While she would think about His mysteries, about the image of God in her life, discussing these matters with Andrzej Iwanowski, Andrzej believed Felix must be constantly thinking about pleasing his wife in the way lucky husbands do. At the flour mill, Felix lifted sacks of durum wheat from a conveyor belt onto a pallet. Eight, ten hours of such lifting, then on the way home thinking about his wife—though thinking could do him no good, Andrzej knew, if Mrs. Podgorak didn't want him.

Yet she was a beautiful woman and needed attention. Perhaps it's me she loves, Andrzej thought. I would like that. I would teach her. I would do this and that to her. Knowing the catechism instructs us to avoid the occasion of sin, he tried not to think like this too much.

Hard work at the flour mill had stooped Felix Podgorak's shoulders. On Saturday, as the millhand, the boy, and others waited to enter the confessional at St. Adalbert's, Felix looked hawklike. You know how a hawk resting in a treetop looks—wings tucked close to its body appearing rounded, stooped. So was Felix stooped.

"What can I do for her, Father?" he asked aloud when the priest came by as he said his penance. "She seems to be drifting from me, flying from me."

"Seek to understand her," the priest told him.

Father has his role, too. Failing everything else, two months before Assumption Day the good priest had presented Podgorak's wife with Reverend Winfred Herbst's *Ready Replies on Religion.* "Something different. Wholesome. No words wasted. Much in little," reads the cover. She delighted in his gift. Apparently, its Ready Reply on "Victim Souls" interested Mrs. Podgorak enough that in late July she read Chapter 19 to Andrzej. According to Reverend Herbst, victim souls are as

old as devotion to the Sacred Heart, and the first of these noble souls thus to sacrifice herself without reserve was the favored

*pupil of the Sacred Heart, St. Margaret Mary Alacoque. It was the
Savior Himself Who inspired her with the idea of being a victim
soul.*

Unfortunately for Magda, she lived too far from the priest's good instruction and kindness. Most of the time, she had only the boy around
the place.

"I want to talk to him and to you every day," she told Andrzej. If
she was busy thinking when he came to do chores, she'd sit him by the
window in the living room where the clock ticked on the table. "Do you
like the name Margaret Mary Alacoque? Have you ever heard it?"

"Yes," he said.

"Are we made in God's image and likeness?"

"Yes." It reminded him of catechism. "Do you think we are, Mrs.
Podgorak?"

When she looked at herself in the living room mirror to ponder
a response, he wondered whether she was secretly watching him. He
wished Mrs. Podgorak knew what he couldn't confess to the priest
about his indecent thoughts. He wished he could tell her the thoughts.
He'd like to hold her, like for her to take him upstairs to the bedroom
where she could soon see how he felt about her. Instead, he listened to
her talk about victim souls most of the afternoon.

Outside the living room window were the brushy woods, then way
beyond was the steeple of the Polish church. If it was hard for Mrs.
Podgorak to live so far from the priest without having him or Andrzej
to talk to, it was okay by Felix Podgorak to live here in an isolated part
of the neighborhood. He'd told Andrzej this after confession. He didn't
dislike neighbors, he'd said. He just figured, Why be near anyone when,
by the way you acted or by what you said, you were certain to disap-
point them? Too bad the railroad was becoming mechanized, Andrzej
thought. Felix Podgorak could have tended the two-storey tower I am

razing with the crew. Felix would have been perfect at the switching tower, a one-person job except when the grain- and ore-shipping seasons are going strong before the Great Lakes freeze up. An employee used to be needed inside the switching tower to issue paper orders for train crews and to switch tracks by means of levers manually linked outside to the switches.

Now with the increased use of two-way radio and the advent of remote-controlled switches, the tower was being razed. It was no longer of use to the Northern Pacific. Andrzej thought perhaps Magda Podgorak was of no use to her husband. She was another who'd disappointed him. Maybe she had done what she could for him and now she was of no use. I could be of use to her, he thought. He wanted to tell her how he could please her, but she didn't let him. She was saying that if Felix desired to abandon her and if—after her abandonment—she could be used by God to ease others' suffering, then she accepted the role.

"I'll give myself, you watch," she said.

"I don't understand," Andrzej said.

"You watch. I pray for everyone. I pray for America. I pray for St. Adalbert's Church, for Father, for you, for Ada Michalski, for Mr. Jaros." She mentioned all sorts of townspeople you wouldn't expect her to talk about. That day when the paper announced that the Polish government was confiscating the property of the Polish church and that Americans had begun hoarding supplies in case of rationing during the conflict in Korea, she told Andrzej that what Reverend Winfred Herbst calls "souls of sacrifice . . . offer themselves, in a spirit of sacred reparation, that the Sacred Heart may dispose of them completely according to Its good pleasure."

That railroad tracks surround and run through Superior was for Andrzej almost as great a mystery as it would be to go upstairs with lovely Mrs. Podgorak. Where did these tracks run to? Where did the stairs lead, to which soft bed in which quiet room? What joy he'd find with the lovely, frail woman in his arms! He wouldn't resist sinning. Steel rails, gossamer strands, the house with mirrors, the mirror in the garage, his feelings for the victim soul, the stairs, the railroad tracks. The world didn't know everything yet.

Two sets of tracks cross east–west and north–south at the forlorn switching tower. Like the Podgorak's house, the tower rose from fields that, especially in winter, seemed to stretch on forever. Andrzej had seen the brass fittings, brass stove, oak wainscoting, solid oak center beam fifteen-inches square, all of it being salvaged by the three-man crew.

On Assumption Day, the gossamer day August fifteenth, after all these things had gone through his head, Andrzej, finished with work and thinking he'd seen a commotion on the tracks, asked, "What's happened there?"

"You mean the silvery gossamers?" people said.

"Haven't you seen? I mean, what's happened on the tracks a mile over? I've been busy. I want to know what the fuss is about."

He learned Magda had taken flight over the Left-Handed River. Red-winged blackbirds and a few crows had begun a commotion when she fell from the sky, if fall she did. One of the men said she hadn't fallen. She'd headed skyward for a moment but almost seemed to have second thoughts and partly glided, partly fell down into the river floodplain. Whatever the truth, the birds' fussing alerted the NP track crew tamping ties by the cemetery. "There. Who is it down there?" the foreman was heard to yell, pointing to the birds.

It was tough getting to her. This same man who swore he'd seen her fly for a moment waded through the swamp. Andrzej heard over and over in the neighborhood how the rescuer had lost his workboots in the peat, how, when the ambulance arrived, the men lowered a stretcher fifty feet to him. "It was a miracle Mrs. Podgorak came back to earth," the rescuer said. "You should have seen her."

"We can be thankful. She's bruised but resting at home," Felix told Andrzej by telephone a few days later. "When they come home, tell your parents. Tell your brothers. Doctor Stack has talked sense into her. Father Nowak has. She'll be all right."

So many rumors swirled around Mrs. Podgorak. Here was the flight of a blessed angel, people said, but if she wanted to be a victim soul, she could become one in safer ways: through charitable works, through penance, through self-denial. That way she could remain alive on earth.

A week later, Felix came to the Iwanowskis' house. This was August twenty-first. When he coughed, it sounded like indigo buntings warbling inside his thick chest. He poured out his heart. "All the time thanking Jesus, she'd tell me Jesus has denied her. This was fine with my wife. Then she could go ahead and be a victim in His service so that Jesus would . . . I don't know what He'd do—I guess she has to find Him even if it means jumping off the trestle . . . ," he said, his voice trailing off.

"But she was flying," Andrzej said.

When his mother left the kitchen where they sat, Podgorak confided in Mr. Iwanowski and the boy, who was almost an adult, that his, Felix's, wife, wouldn't let him see her naked. "Don't look at me! I'm no reflection of God's divine image," Magda would say if he came upon her changing clothes or preparing a bath. "All the time," Podgorak said, "my wife talks about flying." He looked as though he was resting his large wings for his wife's next journey.

Poor, stooped Felix: Andrzej thought he would always wonder about his wife's flight. Having heard her talk for so many months, Andrzej knew she had made the sacrificial flight for Poland, the "Christ of Nations," which has suffered through much of its history but, like Jesus, would come again in glory. She had leapt from the trestle for Mr. Zielinski, dying of heart problems in the East End; for Ada Borski whose son was being shipped to Korea, where things looked bad; for St Adalbert's nuns, who had little; for Eleanor Zekas, who sought a man with whom to share her life. "For my country America, for my countr

Poland, and for You, I will give myself, Dear Lord *Pan Jezu*," she had prayed in the days before her trial flight of 1950.

The next time she left the way Blessed Mary does on Assumption Day, Andrzej was preparing for his class at the vocational school. He'd bought supplies at the dime store and was enjoying a lime phosphate at the drugstore with the money he'd earned in salvage. "You like new flavors, don't you?" asked the druggist who mixed the phosphate around the time Podgorak's wife was flying away from them all.

The husband had stopped for a beer at the Warsaw Tavern and was passing the switching tower on the way home. Only two weeks since the switching station had been razed and already someone had drawn with chalk on the concrete floor. Whoever it was had sketched three birds lifting a woman off of a trestle. Seeing the drawings got Podgorak moving faster for home, which is when Andrzej caught up to him. For the rest of the walk, the boy saw him bend forward every so often and hack and hack until the phlegm in his lungs came up. Ordinarily, Magda would have heard the boy or her husband in the yard, but not on the day she perfected the art of flight.

"She's left me" is all Felix could tell anyone.

She must have been just short of heaven by the time he stepped into the kitchen where usually she'd be preparing his supper.

If they don't know exactly what has happened to a wife who's escaped her husband, then priests can't really pray for her at Sunday Mass. It is not as if she's dead, not as if she's divorced. Yet where is she? Andrzej overheard two young wives wishing they could follow her example. They swore to each other they'd seen her falter momentarily, then rise gradually above the NP ore dock and head eastward over the Great Sweetwater Sea. And that was it. What consternation it caused! Alone her husband prayed for the dear wife who was nowhere to be found.

When September came, he stopped one last time at the Iwanowskis'.

He was selling his house and wanted to say good-bye. With nothing else to do, Andrzej had arranged dry wildflowers in vases. Blue wood aster, heal-all, touch-me-not—they had brightened the fields by the house. Mr. Podgorak's breathing sounded like a bird had gotten loose in the house. He had lung troubles from breathing flour dust at the mill. The hay fever caused by the goldenrod that blooms at this time of year was bothering him. Over the rustling of the curtains blown by the breeze, you could hear him struggle to catch his breath.

"When you breathe does it hurt you?" asked Andrzej's younger brother.

"Yes," replied Felix.

When Mrs. Iwanowski came in with a tray of cups for coffee and saw the distraught widower—for this is what people thought of him as, a widower—she shook her head. He didn't seem to be getting better. On he talked. "Some won't be happy to trust the Lord's word. They want proof of His body on earth. If they don't find it, they have to see for themselves if there is a heaven."

In the living room, shadows appeared that, a week before, weren't there, though it was still early afternoon. Outside, a few leaves on the elm trees had turned yellow. When late summer enters a house, the whistle of trains crossing the Ninth Street trestle sounds lonely in the cool air. The sunlight has a different quality.

Mr. Iwanowski agreed to take the dresser and mirror from Podgorak's garage. He'd store the dresser in his own garage until one of his boys—Andrzej, Lesczyk, Joe, or Maciej, who was deaf and mute—got married and could take the piece of furniture.

"That's settled then," Podgorak said.

As if he could rest now, Mr. Podgorak, exhausted from trying to find his wife, from praying, from confessing to everything he'd ever done wrong, lay his head on the back of the couch. Nodding to her husband to leave the coffee cups on the tray, Mrs. Iwanowski motioned him and the brother, Lesczyk, to come with her into the kitchen. Andrzej, th salvager, remained with the millhand, who slept in lengthening shadows until a light, easterly breeze perfect for spider weblines whispered to him, and he awoke to see the wildflowers Andrzej had moved nearer to him.

"Feels like I slept through September," Felix said, looking as though he'd grown very old. "I've suffered. I want you to see something. Carry the sight with you. Look at it. You salvage things."

Pulling up the white, long-sleeved shirt his wife might have washed and pressed for him before she ran or flew away, he turned his back to Andrzej. From across the room, the boy could see—through the shadows—Podgorak's skin made paler by the color of the shirt, the winglike shoulders of a man who lifted flour for a living. As if every bird in his chest was singing with the effort, the millhand drew a breath. As he did, into his side went a hole. "A war wound from an Italian machine gunner," he said. "They took out the bullet, sewed me up. We were around Rome. Maybe it was a Roman got me."

The hole became deeper when he inhaled again before letting the shirttail drop. "Here, you have this for a keepsake." He handed Andrzej the shell the doctors had given him six years before. "You know what the 'IHS' means on the altar in the church? I sure have found out. Say it and you'll understand. He got me through the war, Jesus did. I don't know if He can get me through this."

"'I Have Suffered'? Is that what it means?" asked Andrzej. He was recalling how hard the work of salvage had been—and now to see a man with his side pierced like Christ's by a Roman. "Does it mean suffering?" Andrzej asked again.

"That's exactly right," said Mr. Podgorak as he rose to go, leaving Andrzej wondering why Jesus had not brought Mrs. Podgorak back here on the white strands for a visit.

The birdlike wife had prayed for so many people that she must have gotten worn out. She'd not been wrong praying for him, Andrzej thought, for he was bothered by his thoughts, especially now that his father had brought the Podgoraks' mirror to the garage by means of a wooden trailer. After Mr. Podgorak had shown him his wound and a week later had left for Hastings, Minnesota, to work in the flour mill there, Andrzej wondered whether he should step before the mirror. It is understandable one so young would not live comfortably with the mysteries of Jesus in His life. Who understands His mysteries in the flower of youth? In the mirror, he at least might see an answer different from what Magda Podgorak had seen. This gave him hope he could understand what had happened to her. "A sign. Please, Lord Jesus, something to guide me," said Andrzej. "I have suffered, too," though what had he suffered but a few splinters from working at the switching tower?

Lighter this time, the bloom, the sign, came one lovely afternoon as if the gossamer lines were falling only for Andrzej. After the scientific explanation in the paper a month before, few people cared about silk strands falling in September. But weblines combined with what he'd read recently in *Lives of the Saints*—that as a nun Margaret Mary Alacoque had had visions telling her to suffer in the name of the Sacred Heart, that "a cult of victim souls suffering self-inflicted punishment became popular in France in the 1700s, then spread to Poland"—these ideas led him to think he could rise to the Sacred Heart's expectations of him.

A sensitive boy given a gossamer sign, once he thought it over, he would tell his parents that the proof of Jesus was everywhere. He'd inform his brother Lesczyk, who drew flowers and birds with pencils and chalk. "Everywhere is God, Lesczyk, I tell you," he'd say. "He exists in the gossamer bloom, in the Northern Pacific railroad tower where the tracks cross, in Mrs. Podgorak who learned to fly, in our priest, in our home. God is here." These things, Andrzej was coming to understand, were mysteries hinting at a larger mystery inhabited by the people here, by the people of the Christ of Nations. The next day, he decided against telling anyone. He'd keep his signs and secrets to himself, suffer them silently, as a victim soul would.

On October eighteenth, his birthday, he first watched the breath of his kisses evaporate from the mirror that had been so close to Mrs. Podgorak's pale lips. His lips might have touched the exact place on the glass where hers had been. Sometime during the day, their lips must have touched, Mrs. Podgorak's and the boy's. By then, Andrzej knew, however, that unlike *her* kisses, his were sighs against a mirror, nothing but sighs, and that tomorrow the mysteries of Jesus Christ would be revealed to us all.

A GUIDE TO AMERICAN TREES

My sister Bożena was a bird. A little older than my brother, Maciej, she'd worked for *Pan* Kapaczynski, a landowner who owned a sword and ten rifles. When *Pan*, or Master, Kapaczynski rode into the fields on his roan stallion, my father and brother would take off their caps and bow to him. "All over Europe is getting worse, Stanisław," *Pan* Kapaczynski would say from astride the horse, his sword hanging from his side, his tall black boots in the stirrups. If it was early February, he might say, "*Świętej Dorocie uschnie koszula na płocie.*" And Maciej, who could still hear and speak, would repeat what he said. "St. Dorothy's shirt will dry on the fence." If *Pan* Kapaczynski said in March before the war, "*Świety Józef kiwnie brodą idzie zima nadół z wodą,*" Maciej would say, "St. Joseph shakes his beard. Winter disappears."

We children would wait for the landowner to draw his sword to practice for war. When he said, "Charge!" we'd run through the barley, my birdlike sister Bożena included. While he rode away to safety with his sword, the ten rifles, and his precious collection of amber, we were to guard his fields.

In September when the war finally came, our sentries were barley sheaves. When the Germans poked around, Maciej was terrified. He wasn't right even before then. In a corner of one hot, golden field,

Bożena, my brothers, and I hid. Mother and Father, who hadn't practiced the war game, hid in another field. Maciej thought winter was
passing. He remembered *Pan* Kapaczynski saying, "A single swallow
does not yet bring in spring."

"Hush," said Bożena. But he wouldn't be quiet. "Hush," she said
again; and he said, *"Jedna jaskółka wie czyni wiosny."* The German sol-
diers were swallows to him. I thought it was a gunshot when Bożena,
who was very strong, struck his ears, and Maciej said then and forever
after, "Oh! Oh! Oh!"

This was in Poland, where things happened that are secret. My sister was the white eagle that saved us, the eagle that is the symbol of
Poland. Now we live in Wisconsin. It is 1952, summer. We have moved
here from the South.

Mr. Harry Rosenfield of the American government, officials of the
National Catholic Welfare Council, and Mr. Ugi Carusi of the Displaced Persons Commission in Washington, D.C., had arranged for
people like us in south Louisiana (where we lived after we sailed into
New Orleans) to come north. The headlines on yellowed newspapers
covering our shed walls tell why we left: "DPs on sugar plantations re-
late shocking grievances." *"Wysiedleńcy polscy podobno spoziewanie
w Louisiane." "Kto i w Jakim celu Wywozi Naszych Wysiedleńców Do
Stanu Louisiana?"* One wrinkled newspaper drawing shows a family
in a flimsy, wooden shanty, bugs crawling in, rain blowing through
it the way rain blows now into our broken shed when the wind howls
off of Lake Superior. Émigrés. *Emigranci.* Not everyone had it bad
in south Louisiana. Dubises, Klacks, Cieslickis . . . they stayed on in
Donaldsonville and Plaquemine.

"It is easier to forgive than forget," Mother says about Bożena these
days. Maciej doesn't feel this way. Because he can't hear or speak, it's
impossible for him to tell us why he won't forgive her, though I know
the reason has to do with what she did in Poland. When her name

comes up, he sees it whispered on our lips. "Bożena, Bożena," and this sets him off against our sister.

We came from Łomza, Poland, to Iberville Parish, then to this East End of Superior, Wisconsin. Here are the world's largest iron ore docks. Here are a cement plant, a flour mill, and a coal dock all on the East End side. More of us Polish people live here than lived in the sugarcane country. In the East End is St. Adalbert's Church, which we attend one thousand miles north of my sister, who's still in Louisiana. Only I, and perhaps Bożena, believe we should have remained at Del Rio Plantation. The rest of the family is happy in Wisconsin. Because we were displaced after the war, because I was smart in school and a good writer, and because I draw pictures of flowers and birds, which people think is strange for an eighteen-year-old to do, I am out of place. I am Lesczyk, the displaced person.

When I ask Ma what she made working as a cleaning lady in Louisiana, she says sixty dollars a month, Father eighty dollars a month for driving a tractor. Andrzej and Józef, my brothers, hung around Evan Hall Sugar Co-op. When I was very young, Maciej, who'd had the trouble in Poland, took care of me. During the commotion of a cane harvest, it would've been dangerous having him around the co-op, even if he was only greasing a tractor or shoveling bagasse, the residue left after sugar is extracted from cane. I am now as old as Maciej was when we left Louisiana.

In the years since then, everyone has forgotten Bożena, who must be sweet from being near Louisiana sugarcane so long. In atlases, books, encyclopedias, I have searched for her, learning in school and from personal reading that the Louisiana state capital is Baton Rouge; that in 1932 Governor Huey P. Long, the "Kingfish," had a new capitol building erected to replace the one on the river; that New Orleans has a baseball team nicknamed the same as the state bird, Pelicans. I know that last year Louisiana produced 20 percent of the country's sugar. I know the Louisiana state flower doesn't grow this far north. With its waxlike leaves, the southern magnolia is fragrant. The air around it is perfumed.

In Louisiana, where fragrant magnolias grow, the atlas says the principal agricultural products are cattle, wheat, rice, cotton, and sorghum. Louisiana has dairy farms, yet some DP families got only a quart of milk a month; others none. The Josefiaks lived on bread and canned soup they put lard into. Mr. LaCoco, boss at their place, Raceland Plantation, charged them forty dollars monthly rent for a wobbly chair, stained mattress, bed, broken picnic table, two drinking glasses, two bedsheets, two blankets. In the old country, the Josefiaks hadn't been farmers. It was hard on them doing farm labor in Louisiana cane-fields—the weather nearly killed them. When the Greyhound bus driver came with the Catholic priests to take them and other DP families away from the plantation, Mr. LaCoco said the Josefiaks belonged to him. No priest had a right to remove them. Even the governor supported him. The bus driver said the furniture the Josefiaks rented wouldn't be worth three dollars if it was sold. "That-all is junk," he said.

This was the poor Josefiaks. We had a radio, an ice box, a wood stove. We got a quart of milk a day. Father was given wallpaper to fix up the place after the Negro tenants left it a mess. There were no Negroes in Poland. We called Louisiana "*Czarny Ląd*, Black Land." Our house was comfortable. Magnolias grew around it. In the library I go to, this book, *A Guide to American Trees*, says the magnolia "prefers the rich, moist soil of swamps and riverbanks, though it is adaptable under cultivation." Its white flowers have dark green, leathery leaves. "The name *Magnolia grandiflora* testifies to the fact that it bears large flowers, 6 to 8 inches across."

I dream of this and of the live oaks at the Pleasaunts' that shaded you when you drove under them. They were planted on either side of the lane. This is called an "oak alley" in the South.

Down in the cane country, the planting season goes from the middle of September to the middle of October; the cultivating season from

February to Bożena's birthday, July 1; the general farm work, or "idle season" when the crop's been laid by, from July to early September; and the
cutting and grinding season from September to December, when roads
fill with trucks rushing back and forth from the canefields to the co-ops.

During the idle season, Mr. Pleasaunt's wife, Judith, came looking
for my sister. We lived a half mile from the house. "I know she's with
him," Mrs. Pleasaunt said. Frightened, Maciej bit his lip, closed his
eyes. My sister with a man, Mrs. Pleasaunt's husband. Was she teaching
him to sing? It was in mid-July Mrs. Pleasaunt got mad, called us "dev-
ils." When Bożena came home down the oak alley, ducking when she
passed the big place, Ma pulled her out of Mr. Pleasaunt's car. He was
our boss. My father cursed him beneath his breath. Seeing the looks on
our faces, Maciej couldn't help what he did. He can't speak words. He
bawled, "Oh! Oh! Oh!" and bowed and bowed.

The screen door slammed. Ma walked Bożena through the house
and out the back. Andrzej was coming home from the sugar co-op.
In Polish he asked, "How come is Mr. Pleasaunt here?" Ma, my sister,
they stood by the well, while inside the house, Pa muttered "*Psia Krew*,
Dog's Blood!" and tapped his fingers on the rough tabletop wondering what to do. Behind Pa's back, my other brother, Joe, made a loose
fist. In and out of it, he ran two fingers. Andrzej caught the meaning.
I suspected what Joe, using two stiff fingers and a fist, meant about
my sister. That is a long time in our family's history to go back into.
Sometimes the years confuse me. In and out of the fist went Józef's fingers as he winked at Andrzej behind my father's back.

When Mr. Pleasaunt came for my sister again, my father followed
the Polish custom. Privately, he cursed the landowner for what he
was doing, but the peasant must bow to the *szlachta*. In America, in
Louisiana, he couldn't break the habit. We are peasants. We are like
the Negroes of Louisiana who removed their hats and bowed when the
boss came to the fields. Even in the North, my father forgets and bows.
Maciej bows. I bow.

Now during the idle season here in the East End of Superior, Mother is angry because I haven't joined my brothers on a farm in the country for summer work and because I haven't cut the weeds in the field that separates our house from the Malmquists'. It's a city full of weeds. In a tiny plot in the Malmquists' field, my father grows potatoes. He has the family's permission. He bows to them in Superior as he bowed to others in Louisiana. He works on the ore dock, grows his potatoes, bows to the Malmquists, to the nuns, to the priest. Unlike my father, the potato grower, my goal is to go back to Louisiana. My parents say I must cut the weeds in their field, as payment to the Malmquists, before the city does and charges them for the work.

If Darla, the Malmquists' daughter, knew her boyfriend, Gerald, was leaving Superior with me, she'd be jealous, fight with him, beg him to stay. It's best to keep the news private between Gerald and me.

In the library, Mrs. Pedersen has the windows open. The small fan doesn't cool her. She is a Swede like the Malmquists. She smells like the floor wax the janitor uses. Every day she wears a white blouse. The rest of her clothes are gray—the skirt, the jacket she buttons in the heat. Her gray hair is pulled back, pinned. In the heat, no one visits her. During working hours, she gossips on the party line. If I talk too loud, she says "Quiet!" There's no bringing Maciej to the library, she has warned.

Studying the atlas, I whisper to myself about Mr. Pleasaunt of Donaldsonville, Louisiana. I press my finger over the town in the atlas as if to erase him from memory. Bożena and Mr. Pleasaunt. In Pa's dictionary when I was twelve, I found words for what they did together. Probably Joe had drawn the arrow in black ink to the words "*obcowanie (z kobietą)* . . . to have sexual intercourse with a woman." The closest I come to a description of myself is "*nieco cudaczny*, a little odd." When the dictionary, *Angielski–Polski i Polsko–Angielski SŁOWNIK* was published, they must not have had people like me in Poland. There is no exact word to describe Lesczyk Iwanowski.

"It's hot weather," I say to the librarian. "I need to check out more books, please."

She doesn't like me, doesn't like my accent. She has lived in the East End too long to let foreign people take over. With her papery fingers, she rolls the pencil with the date stamp on the end of it.

"What do you want?" she asks.

"Please stamp the book," I say. In the library, it is as hot as Louisiana. Standing before her as she picks up the phone to gossip, I check the due date in Mr. Harnett Kane's *The Bayous of Louisiana*. She moves the fan so I get no breeze. "It's that annoying Polish boy I've told you about," she says.

When I hear this, I follow the custom my father did in *Czarny Ląd* when he pressed his hat to his heart and bowed to the landowner. I take the one book she's allowed me (Mr. Harnett Kane's) back to the table.

Darla Malmquist dislikes me more than the librarian does. She suspects something's going on with her boyfriend and me. She won't know where he is once he's left for his Uncle A.J.'s on the Indian reservation in Hayward. He'll meet me in Spooner at the gas station with the wooden Indian head outside of it. On the road map, I have seen a picture of the gas station where tourists go.

"We'll make a good team on the way south," I tell Gerald when he comes into the library.

"Shh!" Mrs. Pedersen says.

"We can try a trip," he says.

Gerald has a stack of magazines the priest at the other Catholic church in the neighborhood loaned him. Dealing with a priest's vocation, they are called *The Franciscans*. The priest at St. Francis thinks Gerald wants to store up riches of the spirit on earth. Gerald is afraid Father Sixtus, a Franciscan, knows he's been violating the sixth commandment with Darla Malmquist. This is why Gerald told him he wants to be a priest and took *The Franciscans*. Besides the house across from ours, the Malmquists have a farmhouse. When he's out there,

Gerald's not thinking of the priesthood. "That's where we swim, in the pool the Poplar River makes. It takes me six strokes to get across it. I have to maybe get into deeper water to get away from here," he says.

When teenagers aren't supposed to talk this way, how do I tell him he's a handsome movie star? He speaks English and the Polish he learns from hanging around the neighborhood. Gerald is best speaking the Indians' tongue. In that language, the Left-Handed River that forms the neighborhood's east boundary is named "Nemadji" River. Wisconsin is their word for "River of the Flowering Banks." Gerald is native to a place where people from other countries have built flour mills, ore docks, and railroad yards.

When I came to St. Adalbert's School, Gerald was first to welcome me, saying "Hello" in Ojibwa. As repayment, I drew him a picture of an Indian paintbrush flower. I have it in the sketch pad I write in: "The Idle Season of Lesczyk Iwanowski." I must write in it that when I wrap *The Franciscans* magazines in cellophane then hide them for Gerald in the Malmquists' uncut field, he is with Darla swimming.

Before I see him again, I've drawn a blue wood aster.

"Why do you draw those things? You draw all the time," he says.

"I want to be famous. We should find my sister. In *The Bayous of Louisiana*, Harnett Kane says water hyacinths are purple with fine-colored green leaves. He says people living on bayous pronounce it 'bi'a.'" I tell him water hyacinths were introduced to America during the 1884 International Cotton Exposition in New Orleans. I think water hyacinths choke the bayous the way the neighborhood chokes Gerald and me. I tell him everything I know about Louisiana.

Is Bożena a water hyacinth, a silky aster? What is Mrs. Pedersen? What flower is Darla? I wonder. I've asked her about blossoms on a bush beside the front porch at the Mrozynskis' house. "What are they? I wish they were magnolias."

"They're mock orange. *Philadelphus*. You're teasing about magnolias. They can't grow here. It's too cold for them," Darla'd said. She is very smart in school. It is like she's broken from a bough, though. Two months ago, apple blossoms on the trees looked like pink snow showers. This was Darla back then. Now she's turned against everyone. She looks as though she doesn't sleep. "Why do you lie?" she asks me.

From farther and farther away, I have heard her ask me, "Aren't you leaving East End?" until, to get free of her, I have had to go to the Mrozynskis' to draw the mock orange.

"I won't leave till I see magnolias," I tell her. "They grow fifteen . . . twenty feet tall. Someone said you were pregnant."

"Why don't you leave? He said you were planning to."

"Gerald's not going to tell you secrets. Don't think he will," I say.

"Shh!" says the librarian when Gerald walks in to plan our route south.

At home, my bedroom is stifling. My brother, Andrzej, once told me Jesus' mysteries appear in East End. I take this into account with the librarian. I observe and sketch her. In my sketch-drawing, she is an angry, secretive woman in gray. I will sketch Darla next. She will be a flower that can't sleep and secretly blooms at night. I know things about nighttime. I have heard my brother cry at midnight because of what happened to Mrs. Podgorak of St. Adalbert's Church. Some say Magda Podgorak was a bird that flew away. My brother did chores for her. I have drawn her in blue chalk on the cement floor of the railroad switching tower that's been torn down. No one saw me working in the moonlight. My sister was a bird. That was in the old country.

When Mother comes into my room, she says, "*Próżnowanie początkiem*—Idleness is the root of all evil, Lesczyk." To describe Darla, she says, "*Kurwa*."

"You shouldn't say that about her," I tell her. It was the word Joe had also called my sister when the sugarcane grower brought her home. Mother thinks our neighbor and my sister Bożena are sinners.

"*Kurwa*," Ma calls Darla again, Bożena, too. It means "whore." "No *goot* pregnant. I am repeat, too, what she says about you, Lesczyk. You want the St. Adalbert's priest knowing I have son like you?"

"What am I like?"

"No *goot*, she is pregnant. You are not what she says, either. None of you is no *goot* if you are so different like that."

"Old women think everyone's different," I say.

"No *goot*," she says and stares at me as though she's discovered something about me she doesn't want to know. Heat makes her say things she'll regret.

The atlas in the library says the July mean temperature is 83.1 degrees where Bożena lives in south Louisiana. Harnett Kane believes piroques travel on dew because they are so light. Outside my window, honeybees buzz in the purple clover. I think we must have five bees for each dollar the Josefiaks paid Mr. LaCoco for Raceland Plantation furniture. Swallows fly into the barn. They irritate and please Maciej. At four o'clock, my father plunks his lunch pail down. He points to the newspaper announcement addressed to property owners, reads it to me: "If a lot contains grass/weeds reaching twelve inches or higher, the city is obligated to cut it and bill you for the service. The city will be mowing lots on or near July 26. Per Order of Weed Commissioner."

"*Tak, tak*, yes, yes," I say to him. After he cleans up and eats supper, he is going to the movies with Mother. It is a movie about Frédéric Chopin.

When they leave, I get the scythe from the back shed. I sweep its sharp blade through the field as though to cut down every memory of people I've bowed to. After an hour's hard work, I know I will have the field cut by July 26. I think of the country of my ancestors, of Count Ogiński's polonaise "*Pożegnanie Ojczyzny*," of Paderewski, of Chopin of General Piłsudski.

"You're doing the field," Darla says. She surprises me. "I saw you parents leave. I had to come over. Are you mad at me, Lesczyk?"

Under her clean, white T-shirt knotted at the waist, her skin is tan. She's brought a wildflower guidebook. She is like a sinful, pretty flower that cannot sleep. She sucks on a stem of clover.

"Things have to be cut. Everything in the field has to go," I say.

"In this heat? Stop and taste the clover with me, then see if you can cut the field. What are these?" she asks about *The Franciscans* magazines Gerald gave me to hide. "Why are they wrapped up? They're for priests."

"I don't want Ma seeing them. Unfortunately, being in the heat out here makes the paper curl up."

"Is this some kind of secret?"

"Father Sixtus pushed them on Gerald. He wants Gerald to be a priest, a monk, or whatever they are. Gerald won't bring them into his house. If Mrs. Bluebird saw the magazines in his room, she'd ask him questions, want him to go back and see the priest. I'm hiding them in the field for him. If she saw them, my ma would ask questions, too. I'll spare Gerald. I'll bring them to Father Sixtus," I say. I take them from the grass I haven't cut, a package of vocations magazines wrapped in cellophane. "Why'd you call me what my ma said you did, Darla?"

"Why do you want Gerald to leave here?" she asks. "He wants you as best man. A chaplet is a wreath of flowers. Gerald has one. I have one. I've made them from the wildflowers out here. The clover smells like vanilla when it's been cut. That's because of a chemical in it."

She reads about the touch-me-not flower. I do not know what it looks like. "'A forward pointing spur hangs nicely balanced on a slender stalk,'" she says. "Is that you, Lesczyk? 'When the mature seed capsule is touched, it explodes in curling segments to scatter its seeds.' Do they have a flower like you in Poland? The touch-me-not?"

In her wildflower guidebook, I see the name again. "Gerald and me are getting out of here," I tell her.

"I'll add you to his wreath," she says. "He wasn't telling me at first, but now I know he's not going to Hayward to A.J.'s and that we're getting married. You two aren't leaving."

"If my dad used more of your field for his garden, I wouldn't have to cut as much," I say to her. I touch her hair. This makes me think of Gerald, who touches her face and hair every night.

"No roof needs fixing at his uncle A.J.'s. That was his excuse to get away. A.J. can wait. Gerald's confessed," she says. "He's not leaving."

"I have to bring the magazines into the house," I tell her.

From my room, I watch her pick purple clover for a chaplet.

"What are you doing?" she asks through the screen. "Your door's locked. I can't wait out here."

"You're wrong about him," I say.

When she crosses the field to her house, I call him. He's leaving with me. Though his line is busy, I know this for certain: he's leaving with me.

Evening slips into the room. It brings the shadows of Poland. The line is busy. Darla has gone home. When the time comes, I'll write my parents a note saying that I've left here to pick strawberries during the harvest in Michigan. *Bożena had to hit Maciej. We'd have been discovered by the Germans. Now Maciej can't hear or speak. He couldn't tell anyone where I've gone.*

Free of the magazines I leave at the rectory, I hurry to a phone booth It is the first glass phone booth in this city. I have two nickels. Inside the phone booth by the Arrow Café, I can call in private without my parents listening. Trapped by the glass door, caught in the light of the booth, moths flutter. I see my face in the glass. I will tell him anything to be loved.

"You're awake," I say.

"I'm studying the map," he says.

"I'm going to be an artist."

The moths aim for the light but are never satisfied. On the phone from Gerald comes a smile I see across the line, a smile lit by the moon

Everything is lit by it. "You're going to hate me. There's no trip," he says. "I'm getting married."

"We're leaving. I wrote it in the sketch pad. I wrote every detail. Why are you saying you're not going? We planned. You don't know what this is going to do. We planned every road."

When he doesn't say anything, I let him know that he'll never see miracles. Despite the things I've promised him on these days and nights before the trip, he's made other plans. He's staying to work on the ore dock where my father works.

When I call Darla to tell her who I have loved on his horse in his high, black boots, I expect her to envy me. But on a night that smells like mock orange, as if moved by the beauty of the telephone confession I am making to her about *Pan* Kapaczynski and moved by the beauty and mystery of her telling me she's having Gerald's baby, she says, "How is it possible when we're so young? How can there be this many mysteries, Lesczyk?"

"Anything's possible. Gerald can wear the wreath," I say to her. "I will keep *Pan* Kapaczynski to myself."

"Are there other mysteries? You're crying."

"Yes."

This is when I tell her what I have discovered: that in the middle of the Malmquists' field where no one but me has seen it is the *Magnolia grandiflora*, Louisiana's state flower, which has grown thirty feet tall, has a lovely fragrance, and has large, waxlike leaves made bigger in the July moonlight.

"You never noticed it, Darla," I say to her on the night of my flowering. "It's the largest tree in the field."

"It's too cold for magnolias to grow here, Lesczyk."

"Not in darkness," I say. "That's something you don't know about me, what I have witnessed in darkness in Louisiana, in Poland."

"What have you seen that I haven't?"

"I can't tell you. I couldn't tell anyone. Besides *Pan* Kapaczynski, who'd believe my secrets? I fought in a war in the dark. I carried a sword in the dark. I drove a tractor through sugarcane in the dark. You didn't see the tree so how could you know?"

"You couldn't have done those things. You were young. You'll say anything to get us to like you."

"I did them. *Pan* Kapaczynski is a count in Poland. He is coming to America."

"You're still crying."

"I have so many secrets frozen in me like amber to keep until he returns. We will ride through East End to you and Gerald with amber for your wedding. We're meeting beneath the magnolia in the field. You can expect us," I tell her. In the reflection of the glass, I see my face wet with tears. I have told her everything.

When I hang up and open the phone booth door, the twilight moths fly out ahead of me. They shoot out like stars, like wildflowers, into a sad night of fragrant leaves, waxlike and secretive.

REPORT OF THE
GUARDIAN OF THE SICK

Al Dziedzic's son survived Vietnam in 1967 by telling himself that things would be different when he got home. Now that the new year had come and he was back in Superior, Pete and his old man, Al, were arguing again, this time over how to clean the claw-footed bathtub. On his knees, Pete used Comet and a washcloth, yet the old man—head buzzing in the bathroom steam—claimed to see rings bigger than the rings of Pluto near the bottom of the tub.

"Saturn," said his son, kneeling by the toilet. He'd been discharged from the Marine Corps and home three weeks, long enough to grow out his hair, which was drying in a towel twisted like a turban. "It's shadowy in here, but your eyes have gone bad if you can't see I cleaned it."

His father was beginning to shrink. To support his back, he'd strapped himself into a beige-colored lady's corset he wore over his T-shirt. Grabbing a lightbulb from the kitchen cabinet, he climbed the chair he'd lugged in. Fumbling with the screws holding the glass globe to the bathroom ceiling, Al unscrewed the bulb, replaced it with a 100-watt bulb.

"See them rings of Pluto in the bright light?" Al said. "Look at the dirt in the tub. It ain't cleaned to my specifications."

"Pass the Comet. You're right," said Pete. To please his father, he sprinkled cleanser again, ran the water, swished it around. A half hour before he was to meet the guys for a night on the town, and here he was in pajamas, the Marine ex-corporal, yellow turban unwinding so he couldn't see what he was rinsing. It was embarrassing for a war veteran not to pass inspection and to have the general walking around the house in a corset.

When Al went into the living room, Mrs. Dziedzic popped into the bathroom to whisper, "I'll do the tub for you later, Pete. Your dad's back's been bothering him." As she put away the supper dishes, she called to her husband, "You rest out there, Al honey. You have to work."

It's not his back, Pete thought, but his lungs that make his life awful—lung troubles and me. The doctor might be right about Al developing osteoporosis in addition to emphysema, but it was worse than that, Pete knew. The old man had mental problems revolving around him, Pete. When he'd missed Midnight Mass on Christmas Eve, that had riled up the old man. When Pete said he hated the Chmielewski Brothers' polka show on Channel 6, that had riled him up. There were a lot of things Al disliked about his son, including the fact that he'd raised a wise guy. When Al was asked at the Warsaw Tavern on a summer day when his pride and joy was returning from Vietnam, he would look up from his bowl of beer, order three pigs' feet, and grumble, "He's coming in the depth of winter." He would repeat the last part in Polish, "*w pelni zimy.*"

But there was this, too: Al going to Communion four weekdays a month to pray for Pete; Al, heart sinking, thinking of his boy and praying when he read in the newspaper of the fighting near Da Nang.

The war the old man had launched against his son long ago was worsening now that Pete had returned from overseas, however. If it wasn't the old bathtub that would never sparkle, the stringy moustache Pete was growing, or the teeth he'd lost in war, then it was the used car Al thought Pete shouldn't own. The Rambler stood beside the garage in a spot Pete had shoveled. The electrical cord from the tank heater under the hood connected to an extension cord he'd plugged into a garage outlet. The car would never start in frigid weather without the heater to warm the engine block.

His own car parked in the garage, rear bumper sticker reading, "YOU BETCHA YOUR DUPA I'M POLISH," Al Dziedzic kept telling Pete in the three weeks he'd been back from Vietnam via Camp Pendleton, California, "It's a waste of electricity having the car plugged in."

But Pete had a good argument: "I'll need reliable wheels if I get a job."

"Apply at the flour mill. There's no place to plug in a car down there. You don't need no car."

"I tol' you I'm not working at the mill. I'll pay you for the kilowatts used on the tank heater," Pete said, but what he offered was not enough to calm the wasps in the laborer's head. Since his son had been discharged from the Marine Corps, Al Dziedzic had begun calling him "*Dupa*, ass."

Eighteen years ago he'd started in on Pete after Father Nowak, a 160 lifetime-average bowler, had told Al, "If you wanted to be happy in life, you should have been a priest like me."

"That ain't a comfort," Al had replied.

Father's words running through his head on a Knights of Columbus League bowling night, Al had missed a 7-10 split. There went the league title, there went the trophy for the Polish parish. He was still teased about it. Not only Father Nowak, but the kids were to blame. The daughter, Polly, and the son, Pete, had put the kibosh on a life of fun. Sure, after he married, Al still had the yearly bowling banquet and his weekly league bowling night to anticipate, but now he also had a wife, two children, and a workingman's house to take care of on East Fourth Street. He'd been free once. If days were long working outside of Minot, North Dakota, or Cass Lake, Minnesota, on the Great Northern section crew, the nights in town—before he'd married Wanda Czypanska—were filled with drinking and dancing. He never thought he'd be trapped by having kids.

Destiny for joyless Al Dziedzic was the dust on his work clothes, the dust on the packing floor of the flour mill, the dust in the water of the slip beside the mill. Sometimes Wanda was dust. The kid was dust, like the time Al had asked Pete, home on leave from the Marine Corps, to wear his uniform and drop by the boiler room. The guys during lunch break would be impressed with Al's son in his forest green uniform with the scarlet chevrons. The kid never showed up while Al ate his meat sandwich, finished his windmill cookies, closed the lunch bucket. But there was also this: Al on the packing floor talking about Pete. No matter how he had it in for him, sometimes Al couldn't help but brag about his son. Then two weeks ago, as if to spite him, the kid had left out his partial plate at the breakfast table.

"I forgot to put 'em in. There are only two teeth in front missing. They made me false ones in Vietnam."

"What happened? Where?" Wanda gasped.

"In war, Ma."

Removing his own choppers to tease his son, to lord it over him, Al, who wouldn't let up, said, "You make your bed, you lay in it. 'All I want for Christmas is my two front teeth.'"

Al, the bitter; Al, the relentless: Wanda cut his hair with electric clippers, washed his blue work shirts, packed his lunch bucket, sent him off with a kiss. When the guys gathered in the boiler room, Al, for forty years now sitting in his white, visored, miller's cap, would open his lunch bucket to see which tidbit Wanda had surprised him with. Once, he'd found a wad of chewing tobacco in an Eddie's Snoball. Thereafter, she bought him Hostess products, Twinkies and the like.

For Pete's part, he'd been getting a solid education from all of this. He was being home schooled before the term became popular. In fact, he was nearing the Ph.D. level of his education. He'd heard the academic term from his mother. She'd completed a two-year associate's degree at the college in Superior. She'd also gotten a certificate in "The Palmer Method of Muscular Movement Business Writing." According to her diploma, she was qualified "to execute successfully this system of Business Penmanship." Though she had two years of higher education, she still called the credential her college professors had a "Ph—" degree.

"What you're saying sounds like an acid neutralizer. You forget the 'D.' Ph.D., Ma. Remember when I'd go to the store? Your grocery lists read, 'Buy titbit for Dad.' That's wrong, too. It's tidbit," Pete said, feeling it was high time for him to do the correcting. If, when he was younger, he'd sneaked a Lucky Strike from Al or disrespected the nuns, he'd have been corrected pronto by the guy who'd left the railroad and who, in deference to his corset, was downstairs complaining, "This thing's squeezing me to death."

"Come up here. I'll tighten 'er for you," Pete said as he looked through his discharge papers. Now with the temperature eight below in northern Wisconsin, he was out of cigarettes, his hair was damp, and the general was bugging him about things beyond his control. Even Wanda said the tub would never look new. At least he was through with the Corps. On second thought, today's temperature at Camp Pendleton might be seventy degrees, he thought.

When he needed to escape the old man, Pete found comfort knowing that Happy Hour runs from 8:00 to 9:30 in the morning at Hudy's Polish Palace, then resumes for two hours at 4 o'clock, though there is little to be happy about during the winter or the spring, which in northern Wisconsin is called "Winter Lite." Say you're looking for Ted Wierzynski, Bernie Gunski, or Joe Novack. By the time you inquire about them at Hudy's Polish Palace, they are heading around the horn for cocktails at other East End establishments, the Warsaw Tavern perhaps, Mr. B's, or the Dirty Shame Saloon. If you escape your neighborhood to stay in drinking shape by having a beer in every Tower Avenue bar in the Uptown three miles away, that is called the "Death March." Few return to a tavern for a day or two after a Death March. Going around the horn in East End takes less out of you. What puzzled Pete as he hurried through the cold to Hudy's was where his father had gotten a corset. What other East End man wore a foundation garment?

Standing before the neon *"Na Zdrowie"* sign, a toast meaning "to drink to somebody's health," Andy "Hudy" Hudacek was finishing a bag of salted peanuts behind the bar. A line of retired laborers slumped before him.

Shivering from the cold, Pete asked him, "How's your nuts?"

"Salty. How's urine?" Hudy said.

"The way you like 'em. I could've been laying in the California sun."

"How's your father?"

"Nie ma Ojca."

"Al's all right," Hudy said, emptying ashtrays. "You shouldn't say that. Sure you have a dad. Don't deny him."

"Beer for all, Hudy, courtesy of the Marine Corps."

In a back booth, two of Pete's friends were planning to join the Polish Club. No one but old relatives—dads, uncles, grandfathers—did this. "We'll go join for a joke," Ted Wierzynski was saying. "First we'll swing past the Accordion Hall of Fame."

During Pete's tour in Vietnam, the Hammond Avenue Presbyterian Church had closed. A lady who loved bellowed instruments had purchased the building. Deconsecrated, the church was filled with accordions, concertinas, button boxes, sheet music. In this way it was made holy as a place to worship these instruments and men like Whoopee John Wilfahrt who'd made them famous. Over the front door, a cement scroll contained a message as appropriate to the new business of accordions as it was to the old one of religion: ENTER THESE COURTS WITH PRAISE.

"You walk here in the cold, Pete?" Bernie Gunski asked.

"Al never let him learn to drive," Ted said. "Pete's the one that doesn't own a car."

"I do now. Look by the garage sometime. Whose car's that, do you suppose? Bob Kiszewski drove it for me last week when I bought it. Pretty soon I'll get a license for the Rambler. Right now I practice beside the garage in a spot I cleared. When the old man's at work and can't see me, I inch forward and backward. I've driven fifteen inches. I know how to work the lights. Ma doesn't tell Al about me sitting behind the wheel practicing."

"You won't have to worry about mileage driving that far," Gunski said. "You'll go six feet in a year."

"It's plugged in and the engine turns over every time."

"I'll buy this round," Gunski said. Unable to walk straight after an afternoon of drinking, he propped himself against the jukebox.

"We need polka," Mr. Pogozalski said.

"You'll wreck the Happy Hour," Pete said. "Play it when I'm not here."

"We've gotta go, Pete. I've picked up our applications. Let him listen to the jukebox," Ted said.

Inside the tavern, "She's Too Fat Polka" was playing. Outside, beyond the glare of the "*Na Zdrowie*" signs at other bars in the two-block East End business district, they could see the arch over Fifth Street the ore dock makes. They could see Eddie Meyer's TV-Radio Repair, Sully's Café, the windows iced over. A train rolled toward the flour mill.

"In Vietnam they had miniature trains. Their cars, their buses, everything else was small. We had a fellow nicknamed 'Head and Shoulders,'" Pete was saying. "He had no neck. His shoulders rose up like I don't know—horns on a cow? You know that Irish guy you see in the East End that has a married daughter and rides the city bus from Billings Park out to visit her? His name is Moriarty like in Sherlock Holmes. He's shameless about farting. People call him 'the Despicable

Moriarty.' You ever heard of a guy in a Polish tavern doing that on purpose? He'll say, *'Erin go bragh,'* and let fly. Sometimes when you're downwind of the fan at the Warsaw Tavern—What do you think my old man is called? I had another argument with him."

"Gunner's passed out. Hand me a beer, Pete."

"No wonder Al can't breathe working in flour dust. He walks around eight hours a day with a vacuum machine blowing dust off of the motors. He blows motors."

"Isn't that a crime against nature?"

"The old fellas work hard," Pete said. "Blowing motors ain't for me."

"Are we here?" Gunner mumbled.

"We must be. The sign says, 'ENTER THESE COURTS WITH PRAISE.'"

"It looks closed. Why's it dark inside?"

"It's a Hall of Fame. Have a beer, Pete. I think I'll have another one, too. Let's go to the Polish Club. This place is shut down for the night."

In the Uptown, they passed the Hub Bar, Flynn's, the Capri. *In the Heat of the Night* was playing at the Palace Theater.

"You know Al's nickname for me? No matter what I do, graduate from high school, join the Corps, build a birdbath, cut the lawn, it's 'Bozo.' Lately he's calling me *'Dupa.'* 'Did *Dupa* wash the car today? Did *Dupa* do this or that?' A bozo's a clown that sits above a tank of water and yells at people to throw a ball at a target and dunk him. Well, I'm high and dry. This Bozo ain't wet. While I was drying my hair at home, I decided I'm reenlisting. I'm going back in the Marine Corps and taking the Rambler. Maybe I'll have a sergeant's stripes the next time we meet."

"Ten beers are too many," Gunski was saying.

"Some night we'll drink twenty beers," Pete said.

When applying for membership in the Thaddeus Kosciuszko Lodge of Superior, you follow certain procedures. First, you fill out the application form as you wait in the bar downstairs. During the waiting period, regular Kosciuszko members sit in the dance hall upstairs. They are following the Order of Business listed in the club's *Constitution and By-Laws*. The Introduction of Applicants for Membership comes late in a meeting after the Treasurer's Report. Twenty lodge brothers scraped their overshoes on the floor, complained about the bitter-cold January.

The dance hall smelled like last year's cabbage, last year's beer and cigarettes. A Polish flag hung on the wall. Dr. Kielbasa, the Wally Na Zdrowie Trio, and the World's Most Dangerous Polka Band had recently held a battle of the bands, and aftershocks were still being felt. After Mass at St. Stan's and St. Adalbert's, the Polish churches, and at St. Cyril and Methodius, the Slovak church—and all day and night in the downstairs bar—people talked about how Wally Na Zdrowie, a local guy, had taken the Polish Club by storm with his hit "I'm from Planet Polka."

At a table before crossed Polish and American flags, Mr. Grymala, the lodge president, said, "Rise please!" when the sergeant-at-arms led the trio up the dark stairs into the hall.

"Citizens, raise your right hands," the vice president said to the three beer drinkers, then read from the *Constitution*: "I call on you before God and before the entire Thaddeus Kosciuszko Society to reply to the following truthfully, for if it should later develop that your statement was made not in accordance with truth, you will be expelled with the loss of all rights and privileges. What are your names?"

"Pete Dziedzic, Ted Wierzynski, Bernard Gunski."

"Ages?"

"Twenty-two."

"Nationality?"

"Polish-American."

"In good health?"

"Yes."

"Are your wives in good health?"

"We're not married."

"Do you promise to abide by the by-laws and constitution of the Thaddeus Kosciuszko Lodge, so help me God?"

"Yes."

To commemorate the occasion, Mr. Grymala gave them a Wally Na Zdrowie record. On the cover was a photo of Wally in a smoky dance hall, one hand on the keys of his accordion, the other pointing to a group of hippies with granny glasses and long hair. "Polka or Get Out!" the words above the photo said.

When new lodge brothers are taken in, applause rings through the old hall. Seeing the solemnity and joy in the workingmen's faces, the boys had sobered up. They swore never again to mock polka. When the clapping died, Mr. Grymala nodded to the guardian of the sick for his report.

"On 12/10," Joe Dembroski, the sick director, said, reading from a sheet of paper, "I visited Frank Rozowski at St. Francis Nursing Home. He's eighty. He sends a hello to us. The next day, I visited George Ham. He slumps in a wheelchair. When English don't work, I try speaking Polish. He's in pain, so I leave him a card for the nurses to read him. I went on 12/11 to see Ed Budnick at his house. He's bothered by rheumatism. I'm sad about your pa, Pete. I visited there, too, before you got to town. He's sick with his lung and his back. I don't know why he works anymore. Al will be proud of you for joining."

"Hooray for Pete and the boys," the members said.

"He'll get a seventy-dollar sick benefit. Your ma and dad, when you were in Vietnam, they didn't want you knowing he missed two months of work at the mill."

"He's crabby as ever. What's wrong with him now? Aren't his dues paid?"

"He couldn't get here to pay them," Mr. Grymala said. "That shows you how bad he was. June was the last time."

When Al was last at a meeting, Pete calculated, he himself had been wading through road dust that rose to the tops of his boots. A fine dust had veiled the blistering sun, and his friends back home were writing him about the cool summer. According to Mr. Grymala, Al had been operated on twice over the summer. No one had told Pete about General Al Dziedzic, the bowling star, and his misery.

"I know it's not much of a sick benefit. Same as in 1928 when the lodge started," the guardian of the sick was saying.

"I'll tell the old man about it. We better get going."

The members shuffled about, coughed. The boys saluted them. Pete heard the president pounding his gavel, heard the low voices talking about Al, heard the jukebox downstairs playing. "Are there additions or corrections to the Report of the Guardian of the Sick?" Mr. Grymala was asking.

The car wouldn't move when Ted started it. It had square tires from the cold.

"It's lousy, nobody telling me. I go to war, get sucker-punched by a buddy, lose two teeth. I come home, Al's after me—clean the tub, don't miss Mass. Can't we get going?"

"It needs to warm up. Don't be mad we didn't say anything, Pete. We knew he wasn't good. Give the car a minute. There, now we're set."

"Can't you floor it? You'd think Wanda would've let me know. Maybe it's only a bad cold he's got. That's it. I can still leave town, drive down the alley, head south tomorrow. When I get to Iowa, I turn west."

"You haven't driven your car two feet," Gunski said.

"When we get to Al's, pull around so I can check the extension cord. Can't you go faster than thirty? I gotta get home to pack. It's a long trip to Camp Pendleton."

Mrs. Dziedzic wouldn't stop crying when he came in. Off and on, she made the sign of the cross, raised her hands to Jesus.

"I heard about it," Pete said.

"He got worse when I telephoned about your reenlisting. He won't go on long. I'll have to look after your dad when he can't walk to the mill."

She'd taken the rosary from the pocket of her housecoat. The beads wrapped around her fingers.

"It's like we're no relation," Pete said. "He wouldn't tell me about the illness. I'm twenty-two years old, a war veteran gone four years. He was at work or the lodge when I was growing up. I never knew the guy."

"He wanted to take you to the Polish lodge," she was saying. "You were too busy for him. Why don't you write him a note in the ovals of the Palmer Method? Say, 'I'm sorry.' Say, 'I'm going to help, Dad. You, me . . . we'll get through it.' Say the rosary with me."

"Where's my shaving kit?"

"At least leave him a note, leave him something," she said. She crossed herself with the crucifix. The beads clicked. "It'll provide him a sign of love. Tell him you joined the Polish Club. Tell him you're not reenlisting. You're staying home."

"I'm not kidding, Ma. Where's my shaving kit? I don't want you criticizing my handwriting if I write him. He never wanted my car here, like parking it will kill the grass."

"It's twelve below. Your father walks home in twelve below zero weather. All his life, he goes to work, sometimes in blizzards."

"I'll write, 'Sorry you're sick.' I've gotta prepare for my trip. When it comes to the Rambler, I don't want trouble. Tell Al I couldn't wait up for him. I've done my part. Here's the note."

"I'll call the flour mill. 'Give your boy the sign he needs,' I'll say. All these days and years I've said rosaries for you and Al, now he's dying the man is dying."

Pete could hear her on the phone. She was sobbing. "He's going to leave for Camp Pendleton. Do something to show your love."

Mrs. Dziedzic could hear Pete, too. Upstairs, the dresser drawer slammed, a wire hanger bounced on the floor.

Looking at the starlit night, Pete remembered that if the sky is cloudless, radiational cooling occurs when warm air escapes the earth. He didn't know why he'd remember this now. The bottom of the window had frost on it. Reflected in the pane above, he could see himself in the uniform he'd put on. He'd been awarded the Vietnamese Campaign Ribbon, Armed Forces Expeditionary Ribbon, National Defense Ribbon, Good Conduct Ribbon, and a Sharpshooter's Medal for qualifying on the rifle range. Through the window he could see someone a half mile away. He could see the moon in the clear sky.

Beyond Pete's mirrored face, beyond it and the Rambler that would start with the good tank heater, beyond the hill on the other side of the ravine where alder brush rises out of snow that contributes to radiational cooling, from out there in the moonlit night, here came the millhand. He'd walked off the job to see the son he'd been battling since he was born. The entire walk home, Al was muttering how the kid was ungrateful, how he might as well leave town, let Al die in peace and the war between them end. But there was this, too: Al recalling how he and Wanda had prayed their son would be safe in Vietnam when he'd gotten his orders.

As Pete looked out the window, wondering what he'd done to deserve such a father, it seemed to him Al was frozen in time, but he couldn't be, for he didn't have a moment to spare on this January night. He'd passed beneath the Second Street viaduct. Who else would be on the tracks down there but a fellow on the way home from a lifetime at the flour mill? Each step brought him closer to the end of his life, thought Pete.

For a minute, he lost sight of his old man as Al, deep in thought, walked down the alley, passed behind the garage. How many times Al had yelled at Pete, and the boy at the old man. There would be no sign from the old man, Pete realized when he lost sight of his father. There never had been a sign. If it wasn't the tub, it was something else. Thankfully, with the car he had a way to escape. He'd never come back. He'd reenlist for six years, then eight more. When he got out, he'd be a master gunnery sergeant, a lifer. Who cared about anyone back here? His dad could have the Wally Na Zdrowie LP.

"He's coming, Pete. Dad's on his way to rescue you. He'll save the family," Wanda called from the downstairs hallway.

Then there he was again, good old Al Dziedzic, the laborer, back in view the way he'd been in and out of view all of Pete's life. Wanda was right. There was the former Polish Club president, the former Tuesday night bowler, the former railroad hand, and parish council member of St. Adalbert's. Somehow he'd made it from the mill to the car in the backyard. Pete couldn't deny what he was seeing. There he was circling the Rambler, the old man Al Dziedzic, stooping with his remaining strength to unplug the extension cord to keep his son with him until they both died of the wounds that had been inflicted over the past twenty years.

THE SHADOW PLAYERS

Pete Dziedzic's teeth lay buried a half mile south of the Da Nang Air Base. There the lance corporal had quarreled with a private over who'd recorded "Sea of Love." Guys in the outfit were singing along to Armed Forces Radio when Pete said, "That singer's from the northern U.S."

"He's from my hometown," replied the private.

"No, he ain't," Pete said.

"Everybody's proud of him in Lake Charles. His name is John Phillip Baptiste, though on the record he changed it to Phil Phillips with the Twilights."

"You're wrong."

"*You're* wrong," said Private Abadee, hitting Pete so hard he swallowed one tooth and felt another dangling by a bloody thread.

"Give it back to him," yelled the guys, but instead the lance corporal asked for a towel to spit blood into. He was on "Fifth Street," "Queer Street." Rocked by a punch, prizefighters dwell here when they hang on the ring ropes trying to remember who they are. Staring at his flak jacket and M-14 on the wooden floor of the strongback tent, he took a laminated holy card with the Virgin's picture from his wallet. "Hail

Mary," he prayed through his bloody lips as the guys sang, "I want to show you, h-o-o-w much I love you."

The next morning, Lieutenant Sardelli assigned a jeep driver to take Pete to the medical unit on the other side of Division Ridge. The driver wouldn't talk to a guy with no fight in him. Besides, the beauty of the limestone cliffs left them speechless, especially where tatters of silky mist hung from the quiet slopes. This was Vietnam: mists, black-pajamaed peasants planting rice, red laterite roads, monsoons, dry spells.

At the medical unit, helicopters swept in from a combat mission near An Ho. Men hollered, lifted stretchers, held IV bottles over wounded marines. Nurses ran out to help them. It was no place for a person without courage.

In a part of the compound far from the landing zone, the navy dentist looked up. Today's helicopter wounded weren't worried about plaque buildup, so Lance Corporal Dziedzic had saved the dentist from a boring day. Seating him in a chair, the dentist worked the tooth out of the lance corporal's mouth, packing the area with gauze to stop the bleeding. Eventually, the gums healed. Three weeks later, Pete, who'd prayed over and over to the holy card, opened the screen door and took a seat to have a clay impression made of his upper gums.

In a few weeks, he had his teeth. They were bonded to a pink plastic form. The partial plate hooked to the back of his real teeth by means of curves in the bottom ridge of the plastic. The two false teeth fit into the slots left by the original teeth. Because the partial could be flipped in and out with the tongue, it was called a "flipper."

"Bite carefully. When you take it out, put it in a cup of water," said the dentist.

Because of the newness of the partial, for a week Pete was nervous about it. His hands had also shaken two months earlier. With everyone anticipating *El Cid*, the first movie during Pete's tour of duty, a jittery marine, thinking he'd heard movement on the camp perimeter shot up the darkness with a machine gun. This was the big one, Pete had thought, as guys scrambled for helmets, flak jackets, rifles. As it turned out, the company wasn't being overrun by VC. Ending up on Queer Street and losing two teeth was as bad as it got for the young man who'd rise to the rank of corporal before coming home, honorably discharged, to argue with his father in the middle of December.

What had happened to his teeth puzzled him when he finally made it home from the war zone. The lieutenant had wrapped one in tissue paper and, putting up a hook shot, tossed it into the wastebasket. Pete remembered a tooth resembling a lover's teardrop. Because he'd swallowed the other tooth when Private Abadee hit him, that one must have been voided into the outhouse, the four-holer at the compound. Periodically, lime was poured over the contents and the outhouse returned to use. Seven or eight months later, the slanted roof, weathered boards, crude screen door, and plywood seat were doused with kerosene, burned, then covered with dirt and a sign put up: Head Closed.

One discarded in the garbage, the other buried in the dirt beneath the outhouse—the teeth were a part of the history of war. If buried teeth do not decompose, they are resting in the tropical earth beside a scrap of screen and a metal bracket from a charred outhouse door. Someone who had all his teeth and who'd not been to war might have wondered about other things during those days—who, for example, ended up with his Joan Baez albums or what time his fellow protesters were meeting for a drink at the Ramble Inn. In addition to the piastres Pete had spent drinking at the Da Nang Hotel on the afternoon he'd had liberty during that war year, he'd left two teeth in a country 65,948 square miles large.

In the friendly territory of the East End of Superior, Wisconsin (approximately two square miles), he'd lost even more. First, his girlfriend, Cynthia, had slipped away from him. Then his father began leaving without Pete's discussing important matters with him. The girlfriend's departure was tough, but his being on active duty for four years had gotten to her. One night, she'd met a guy at the Purple Onion. "He looks like you, Petey," she'd told him when they bumped into each other outside of the East End Drugstore. Pete thought she was as pretty as ever. He wished they were back in time four years.

"I'm home. Now what am I supposed to do with my life?" he asked. "I haven't seen you in a year."

"Dale works at Water, Light, and Power. Have you learned to drive? Have you got hair on your chest yet? You were twenty-one the last time we met."

"I bought a car. I parked it in the snow beside the garage. I take the driver's test tomorrow. It's my second try. No wonder my old man calls me '*Głupiec*, Blockhead.'"

"Good luck. Sometimes you fail the driving test. You'll make it this time."

"I better be able to drive. Dad is sick. He can't go anywhere. I have to do things for Ma."

"Your poor father."

"I'm back in my old bed. My sister teaches grade school in Shawano, doesn't get home much. I see the guys for a beer. What else is new?"

"Don't blame me for marrying. You were gone, Pete. It was too long to wait."

"You're hitched. That's what I hear. I was gone in Vietnam. I like your parents."

"I like yours. Never blame your dad for anything in life, Pete. Say hi to your mother for me, and to him."

"He's next to go. It's funny. He was always on me. 'Cut your hair. Help with the dishes. Do this! Do that!' I feel terrible for fighting with him. Why'd we always argue?"

"Can't you ask him?"

"It's too late. The doc says he's dying."

Fortunately, Al stayed alive long enough for his son to talk about shadows. After Al drank a small cupful of morphine, when the old man

was woozy but free of pain, Pete would begin the game. Morning sun-
shine on beige wallpaper is perfect for making silhouettes with your
hands and fingers. "What do you see, Pa?"

"A camel's head," Al responded.

"No, a serpent. Try this."

"A duck."

"Good one. And this?"

"A cat."

"Excellent."

"I want to rest now," Al would say after a moment and turn his head
from the wall. Seeing two days' growth of whiskers on his father's thin
face, observing Al's fingers twitching from the morphine as though
practicing the silhouettes he'd later stump his son with, Pete would
get up from his chair. "I'm going out," he'd tell his mother who busied
herself in the kitchen.

Where they lived, February is the sunniest winter month. At eleven
in the morning if you want to clear your head of the shadows your father has made for you, you can walk down Fourth, Fifth, or other East
End streets that parallel the bay in Superior, Wisconsin. Confine the
walk to between Twenty-fourth and Twenty-sixth Avenues, and you'll
see elms, cottonwoods, willows, red osier dogwood, and alder brush
casting shadows along the snowy hillside above the creek. The inter-
weaving shadows of the cloudless days appear to long for someone. For
what reason do the shadows of Superior, Wisconsin—or the mists of
the Annamite Mountains of Vietnam—exist except to remind a marine and his Vietnamese counterpart that the shadows and the mists
were there when they were boys?

In Al's shadowy room, the February light grew dim when the sun
passed west beyond the window. Except during the shadow game, Al
didn't talk. "Check his wristwatch, Pete. See is it keeping time for him."
"Yes, Ma. We're still okay on the time," Pete said. Wanda brought her
husband a can of protein drink for supper, solid food being difficult for

him to swallow. One day a priest brought Al supper. Stomping his overshoes on the back porch before entering the kitchen, he said, "Peace to
this house." "And to all who dwell therein," Wanda replied as Father
sprinkled her with holy water and caught Pete with a sprinkle as he
walked in.

Wanda had covered a TV tray with a lace doily. Next to the can of
protein drink Al would have for supper, Pete had placed, in the form
of a cross, two sticks of red osier dogwood. This scarlet bush grows all
over the fields and woods around Superior. He thought his dad might
be receiving what is called the viaticum (the Holy Eucharist given to
a dying person) in the form of the protein drink—which explains the
wood cross: Pete hoped the cross sanctified his father's supper. In addition to evergreens and the moss that grows dark green in winter, the
branches of the red osier dogwood give color to a snowy country.

If a dying person, whose pale skin resembles snow, is not up to it,
the Church allows someone to say the confiteor "in his name." This
Wanda did for Al, whispering, "I confess to Almighty God, to Blessed
Mary, ever Virgin, to Blessed Michael the Archangel, to Blessed John
the Baptist, to the Holy Apostles Peter and Paul . . ." Then Al sipped the
protein drink the priest handed him.

Father Mike enjoyed a can once he had ministered to the retired
millhand. "Refreshing," he said. Having praised God for His plentiful
gifts, including protein drinks, the youthful priest promised to return
in a day.

When he left, Al reached for his teeth. As if uncertain whether he
was still on earth, perhaps in Vietnam where his boy had been, he
moved one hand tentatively, dreamily, over the blanket, then over the
tray, looking for the teeth, but Al's uppers rested in a cup of water in the
top drawer of the bedside table.

"You put them in for him, Pete."

"No, you put them in, Ma."

"Please, son, you have teeth missing. You know how to do it," she said. Wanda was crying.

Though Al lay in shadow, his son, wanting him to look good in heaven and realizing there'd be no talking about the past now, no apologizing for anything Pete had said or done to him, gently opened his father's mouth and put in the teeth. The mind is funny. Though this was no place for it, Pete found himself thinking about his own lost teeth.

There is an icon that is holy to Polish people. In Buffalo, New York, and Scranton–Wilkes-Barre, in Cleveland, Hamtramck, Chicago, Superior, the Poles keep Her image in their homes. They do this in Kraków, Łomza, Warsaw, Katowice. The Madonna in the icon wears a golden crown. Angels hover about it as they do on either side of the bejeweled crown of the Christ-child the Madonna holds in Her arms. Two scars disfigure Her right cheek. The scars, wounds that have saved the Polish nation over and over, were the work of seventeenth-century Swedish invaders who, after slashing Her beautiful face in a monastery, witnessed the icon's face bleeding and crying. Falling to their knees stunned, the Swedes retreated from the monastery at Jasna Góra, and Poland was saved. The Madonna's picture at Al and Wanda's had been reproduced on quarter-inch-thick wood, seven inches wide, ten long. A paper label on the back read "Made in Poland."

"Are you in pain again, dear Al?" Wanda asked her husband. "Drink this."

When he saw his father disoriented from the medicine, Pete lit the holy candles by the bed. He would practice his silhouette-making against the holy candles' light.

His face washed, teeth in, Al, having drunk the morphine, said, "Let me play for real tonight. That's a dog in the shadows on the wall."

"Yes, it's a dog," Pete said. "Does this look like an alligator?"

"Alley-gator," the old man said. "I hear someone crying."

Pete reshaped his fingers.

"A house, Father? A house like ours?"

"Cat."

"Right again."

"What's that on the ceiling?" asked Al.

"It's just evening," said Wanda. "The morphine makes you imagine things. You thought it was a butterfly. No one's crying."

This time Pete went out on a limb to trick him. He formed his hands and fingers this way and that. A crown in a flicker of candlelight is not easy to make. Nor is the Christ-child. Nor are a mother's scars. The morphine eased Al's pain, as he lay watching. The room was silent as it should be when Jesus and Mary enter.

"What are you trying for now?" asked Wanda. Outside, the early-rising moon had brought shadows back to the hillside. "What is so hard for you tonight, Pete, like you are a craftsman in the old country?"

"I'm trying to solve shadow problems."

In the basement the furnace came on. The warm air blowing through the vent shifted the holy candles' light so that Pete had to re-adjust his hands and fingers. "It's the draft doing this," he said. Try as he might, it was impossible in the shifting light to show them what he wanted—the Polish flags, the white eagle symbolizing that nation, the words "*Pod Twoją Obronę Uciekamy Się,*" which translated mean, "To Your Protection We Flee." All of these things are on the icon of the Blessed Mary and Her Son.

"I think Dad knows what I'm trying to make," Pete said. "How do you know it though, Al? Tell us, when it's the first time I've tried forming this outline on the wall. Do you see it too, Ma?"

"Is it St. Adalbert? Is it St. Jadwiga?"

"No. Try someone else."

"Is it the dome of the Basilica of St. Josaphat in Milwaukee?"

"No, Ma."

"Is it a glider airplane? Is it a Polish soldier charging a tank?"

"Try harder. Look at the wall. Can't you see it in the outline?"

Making the sign of the cross, she knelt by Al's side, whispering the Polish words Pete was trying to read from the icon: "To Your Protection We Flee."

Given the seriousness of his condition, Al Dziedzic had not been restricted as to how much painkiller he could have. His hands rose into the air as if he were holding a chalice of wine, a wafer, a cup of morphine. In the half-light, his hands ran gently over something only he saw. Maybe a veil. Maybe a scar.

Trying to steady them, Pete took his father's rough hands.

"Why are you crying?" Al asked his wife and son. "Is it for me?"

"Who is? Who do you see? Is She in here crying?" Wanda asked.

"He's okay. He's doped up, Ma."

Pete ran his fingers over hands that had swung sledgehammers, hefted railroad ties, run conduit beneath a flour mill floor, accepted the Eucharist at Mass. The son's hands weren't tough from work. In the past months, he'd done little more than make outlines on a wall. He was nothing like his father.

He guided Al's hands down, knelt beside him. With his own hands calming his father's, Pete couldn't make the Virgin Mary's silhouette. He hadn't practiced enough. But this was only a silhouette, after all, and insubstantial. It didn't matter that Pete couldn't make it. Because when Al said something in Polish that sounded like "Holy Mother," Pete knew, as did Mrs. Dziedzic, Who had entered the shadows of the bedroom to match his father's suffering with Her own.

THE CASE FOR BREAD
AND SAUSAGE

When our priest has a stroke, the nuns lament what God has done. *"Jezu, Maryo, Józefie!"* they say as they clasp their hands and look heavenward for guidance. In the bakery and butcher shops, people order sausage, poppy seed cake, and extra bread to help them through the period of great trial. At St. Adalbert's grade school, children cry over the news about Father.

When he is well enough to come home from the hospital, his middle-aged niece and housekeeper, Lu, sits him in a lawn chair on the rectory's front porch. Lu takes this worse than anyone. To keep off the chill, she has dressed him in a car coat and snap-brim cap, then ducked into the rectory to pace back and forth. If you are brave enough to ride past on your bicycle, you see Father helpless, and Lu staring through the picture window. Maybe he waves or says something you don't understand. Then he starts crying from the stroke.

"The Lake Superior wind makes our eyes water, not Father Nowak's condition," I say to Wally Moniak so we will not be embarrassed about the tears in our own eyes. We are on the way to serve Mass.

"I'm crying because I'm hungry," Wally says. He has large, round, dark eyes and pale skin.

"I'm hungry, too," I say. "When I left home, my dad was finishing breakfast. We can't eat because we're receiving Communion. On second thought, I'm not sure I want Communion. Do you think It will fill us up?"

"You know how tiny the Host is," he says.

"How bad do you feel about Father?"

"I feel awful," he says.

Nobody notices when Wally and I use Polish words. For a joke, we call each other *"gówniarz . . . dung-farmer, filthy man."* Our families have lived here forever. *"Dzień dobry,"* he says to old women passing us on the way to St. Adalbert's on the Feast of the Sacred Heart.

Wally and I are in no hurry. It isn't fun serving Mass for the priests the bishop sends to replace Father Nowak, especially when we know that by the time Mass ends, Father will be bundled up on the porch on this cool June morning, and Wally and I, trying to avoid him, will pretend not to see him. The best priest in the world, Father has served St. Adalbert's Parish for forty years. He's kept Masses short, gone easy on penance, come into our classrooms for spelling bees, pitched to us during recess, given us money, and given us half the day off on the Feast of St. Joseph. Seeing him cry, my pal and I will have to turn away.

It's worse when Father's not crying. Then he just stares as if he doesn't know who he is, but is certain you've come to help him. If we could just see him like he was. If an angel could whisper to him, "You are Father Nowak. This is St. Adalbert's. Do you remember now? You came here from Toledo in 1918," then we'd feel better.

"By the way, *Gówniarz*, we're not going home after Mass," Wally says to me when we get to church. "Lu called. We're serving another Mass, one at St. Adalbert's, one in the country. Ma broke the news about the doubleheader. We won't eat for hours."

Coming up behind us, Mrs. Stasiak says, "Who ees thees *Gówniarz* you call him?"

I point to Wally. He points to me. She shakes her head, hurries on

She cleans the church and has her rags and cans of Ajax, "the foaming cleanser." Out of her cloth bag, a toilet brush peeks.

"That could be considered a concealed weapon," I say when she's out of hearing. Wally's in no mood for jokes. "Why does Lu call me to serve Mass?" he asks. "She could get other people."

"Because you're *Gówniarz*, the dung-farmer."

"I'm tired of being him. You're him, too."

Making the sign of the cross with holy water from the font, we proceed down the aisle between the pews of old, whispering ladies. If we're insincere in our bows and genuflections, Mrs. Stasiak will use the toilet brush on us. Kneeling before the Communion railing, we cross ourselves and head into the sacristy. Once we are in cassocks and surplices, we will light the altar candles.

Until we hear his rustling, we aren't sure what's going on in back where Father Nowak's vestments hang in a plywood closet against the wall. Hearing us, a man opens his eyes. "Too much altar wine last night," he says, shaking his head to clear it. "Tough way to make a living. I couldn't recommend it to you."

He is huge. When he comes out of the shadows, he opens his eyes halfway as if he's too lazy to do more. Everything is triple-sized about him. He resembles my favorite wrestler, Bart the Shrouded Sufferer. When I notice the beer smell on him, I think how a person could tuck a sign that reads "*Na Zdrowie*" into one of his three chins. Still, he is a man of God.

As we help dress him for the altar, Wally and I yank in front and back to get the chasuble over him. In the censer we use for the Benediction of the Blessed Sacrament, the priest puts out another cigarette. We doubt he'll make it up the altar steps, but when he does, he begins Mass, "*In nomine Patris, et Filii et Spiritus Sancti. Amen.*"

By the confiteor, when a person strikes his breast and confesses "I have sinned exceedingly in thought, word, and deed," I am so hungry I forget the new priest and my sins. My hunger grows during the kyrie, the "Glory Be," and the offertory. Thinking the Host might take the edge off of this hunger, I decide to receive Communion, even if It can't fill me as much as a Ritz cracker.

When the priest prepares to give Wally and me Holy Communion, saying "*Corpus Domini nostri Jesu Christi . . .* ," how do you confess you're grateful Jesus died long ago so you can at least eat something on a morning in 1958? To feed his flock, the Lord must have to spread Himself pretty thin. In trying to understand what's haunted me for so long, in trying to make the case for bread, I believe I can say the wheat of the Host satisfies our physical hunger a little. This might be the one thing about the Eucharist I understand. Trying to prove the theory, I say, "May I have another Host?" as the priest places the ciborium back in the tabernacle, but he frowns at me, wondering why I'm being stupid.

After Mass, Lu gives us the lunch she's prepared for us. She dislikes the substitute priests as much as we do. She thinks no one should take over for Father Nowak, even after he's had the stroke. St. Adalbert's has always been Father Nowak's territory. Thinking of him, Lu had to make lunch or go crazy, which might be a concept to remember—how bread can keep us from dwelling on the problems of life. Bread and sausage can occupy our thoughts. This makes two points I've come up with about food and the Sacrament.

It is thirty-two miles to the mission at Dedham. The mission is called this not because it serves Indians but because there aren't enough parishioners for a priest to be stationed there. When Father Nowak took us to the mission before he got sick, we never went hungry. He made sure we ate even if it meant not receiving the Eucharist.

The new priest is different than Father Nowak. During the first Mass, he had a hard time kneeling, getting up, then holding the Host aloft during Its consecration. He was probably thinking if this is what took to get a glass of wine, then he'd say a Mass. Something else distinguishes him from Father: with a name like Hemerling, I don't believe the priest is Polish. Now he squeezes himself into the Ford Fairlane.

Wally and I believe Lu was right when she said her lunch would be worth our trip. Heading into the country on mission work, fasting and abstaining all the way, I think of what she's made for us to eat. At the creosote plant, guys are on midmorning break drinking coffee, eating snacks. When we get to the mission, all during the Mass attended by ten faithful Catholics in four rough pews, I dream of a lunch of Polish sausage and ring baloney.

During the introit, camouflaging a whisper behind the sign of the cross and a bow, I say to Wally, "I'm sure there are doughnuts, too." When the priest reads out loud, "My heart is become like wax melting in the midst of my bowels," I cannot look at Wally. I know he'll be laughing. We can't help giggling at words such as "bowels." The Latin words the priest says remind me of food. "*Dominus vobiscum*" sounds like "*Dominus* Nabisco." "*Oremus*" sounds like "Oreos."

After we snicker at "*Homo*" in "*Et Homo Factus Est*," the Mass drags until Communion. Though I wonder whether he means it, Father Hemerling says, "Lord, I am not worthy that Thou shouldst come under my roof . . . ," and everybody repeats it.

Judging from the looks on their faces, the worshippers lining up to receive the Sacrament are hungry. When I hold the paten—a thin, gold plate meant to catch tiny crumbs from the Host—under their chins, I see how much longing they have for the Eucharist that fills them in a different way than it fills people like me. It's a mystery what my grandma or Mrs. Kosmatka, my neighbor, get from It. In their case, I wonder if it has something to do with what they remember from Poland.

When we're supposed to be praying, I signal to Wally as if to say, "How much longer? I'm nearly dead from starvation." Deriving nourishment from the Host dissolving on his tongue, he nods to give me courage.

When the priest zips through the final prayers, the blessing, and the last Gospel, I know it is over. With everyone gone home, I think he will let us eat. Still in his vestments, he hands Wally "*Gówniarz*" Moniak the cruet with the water that wasn't used during the transubstantia-tion, when water is poured into the chalice to mix with wine poured from another cruet. Next he pushes by me like I am his opponent in the wrestling ring. Walking behind the mission, he lights a cigarette.

"I'm starved," I tell Wally. "Don't let him keep us from what Lu packed."

Wally stops me from opening the cooler, though. "Sometimes mis-sionaries go hungry doing mission work. It ain't right to eat before a priest eats," he says. "Father Nowak wouldn't approve of it. Don't wor-ry, the Polish sausage will stay warm."

"But he's having a cigarette. I've got to eat. Why are you sure we shouldn't get going on it?"

"After receiving Communion, I can't let us eat. It wouldn't be right," Wally says.

"Then heck with being missionaries. I just received Communion, too," I tell him. "What kind of priest doesn't care about the suffering? The sins we study in catechism are on display. He's not Father Nowak. We don't owe him anything. Who'd you rather be, Father or this guy who's so big he blocked our view of the tabernacle?"

But Wally doesn't have to stop me. Returning to the car, the priest says, "Help me out of these damned vestments."

We let him place them in the trunk of the Fairlane himself. After he's held out his hands for Wally to pour water from the cruet over them, the priest says, "Now the cooler. Move it up front, and you smart asses jump in back."

Gunning the car out of the driveway, he heads down the road.

"Father," Wally says, "are you Bart the Shrouded Sufferer?"

Admiring the sandwich he's taken from the cooler, the priest says, "Turkey. My favorite. No, I'm not the Sufferer, but I know the Sufferer. He was with me in the seminary in Milwaukee. We were all there, Haystacks Calhoun, Killer Kowalski, Baron von Raschke. Jesus Himself." Tearing off the crust, which he sets on the dashboard, he bit into the sandwich. Several bites later, he tosses the remaining bread out the window, grabs another sandwich. "Are there any pickles?" he says.

I feel my stomach drop. I bet Wally regrets keeping us from eating when the priest was having his cigarette. I think of Father Nowak, frail on the porch, think of his suffering, think of how this priest lies about the wrestlers and is practicing in reverse one of the Seven Corporal Works of Mercy—to feed the hungry, mainly himself.

"I'll eat up everything!" he says as I sink deeper into the back seat. "No, I'm teasing. There'll be plenty for you boys." Nibbling a few small items, he digs into the sausage next. He doesn't finish until he's eaten six smoked sausages plus whatever else was in there, ring baloney or whatever it was.

"Can Ted and I have those crusts, Father?" Wally asks him.

"They might be dusty from the dashboard, but sure. Here you are, Smart-Ass. Eat up."

It's best to respect a man of God, I know. "*Aż was, zjadacze chleba—w aniołow przerobi*, You lowly eaters of bread will be made into angels," our parents would say. The priest would probably agree. Lowly eaters of bread? We eat dirty breadcrusts, Wally saving one in his shirt pocket. The thought of a crust of bread offers little consolation to two missionaries. Maybe this is how the Host feeds the spirit—by making us long for It. The Eucharist means longing. I've heard Mrs. Iwanowski, a Displaced Person lady, say that when her family was passing through Russia, starving, she'd lost hope of ever seeing bread again. She called it "holy bread." I have read that my ancestors came to America from Poland "for bread, *za chlebem.*" If I drop a piece of bread at home, when I pick it up, Mother makes me kiss it. I think I know how Jesus went forty days and nights in the wilderness without food and how Father Nowak went forty years at St. Adalbert's Church giving everything he had to others. They longed for us to be saved, and Father longed for the Eucharist, too. That he didn't finish his work around the parish—this maybe is why he cries so hard on the porch.

"Now look," says the priest who knows Haystacks Calhoun and many other wrestlers from his seminary days. With his thick fingers, Father Hemerling snares dessert. Wiping his mouth after eating the sausage, he says, "You share what's left. *Dominus Vobiscum*, The Lord be with you. I got a lunch later with Killer Kowalski."

Sitting forward to investigate the cooler, we see nothing in it but the flat, white bottom. Going through a day's worth of food, Father Hemerling has eaten his way back to the East End of Superior.

Checking his watch, seeing he's late for his engagement, he drops us off at the rectory, then peels out, startling Father Nowak on the front porch where Lu has parked him in his wheelchair with an army blanket over his shoulders.

Not wanting to see our old priest in his sad condition, Wally and I yell to each other, "Go!" and start to make our getaway for home and our mothers' good cooking. But we stop after a few steps because Father Nowak is crying, saying he is hungry.

"So are we," we tell him, Wally pulling the breadcrust from his pocket.

When we go up on the porch and feed him bit by bit of the crust, Father Nowak calms down. Because we've come over to him despite his sadness and confusion, maybe he senses we will someday be good men who practice the Seven Corporal Works of Mercy. Lu can't believe the change in Father Nowak until Wally and I point to the white crumbs on his car coat and tell her through the window that, lowly eaters of bread, we are feeding the hungry.

A WALK DOWN
LONELY STREET

After the toilets have a workout at the parish fair or someplace, it's fine if I get sick defumigating them. What does he care if I cough out my lungs? My right lung's worst. He is boss and owner of the portable toilet business. Now when my lung feels okay and I itch to get out of the house on Friday nights, I have to sign a sheet he calls "the Honor Code."

"You know the rules, boy. On top of the icebox is the sign-out sheet. I see you're trying to make your white overall jacket into a jumpsuit."

"Yessir."

"You wet the bed last night? No twenty-three-year-old wets his bed. Your room stinks. Do I have to call you 'Sissy-Baby-Bed-Wetter?' We have indoors toilets. If you're uncomfortable with indoors plumbing, and you can hold it in long enough, I'd appreciate you to use one of the units in the yardful of portable toilets outside, so long as you clean it out."

Coughing, I say, "I can't help it if I have a nervous condition."

"That don't qualify nothing. No sir. You'll have to buy a new mattress if you wet yours again. You signing right this time on the sign-out sheet? No such a person lives here as you imagine you are. When you're out, pump Simoneux's septic tank, give Ducarnou's a pump. See you're back early with the truck."

On the sign-out sheet going back to December when I got pneumonia from the methanol I poured in the portables during a cold snap, I write my true name: "Thomas Dugas, March 18." As I head for the truck, I look through the screen door at the kitchen table where he sits calculating figures about the toilet business. Hearing me cough, he shakes his head. Disgusted as he points to me, he says, "I guess other people's shit is my business."

"Oh now, Louie Guidry, don't call my boy that," Ma says.

"Damn right I'm your business, Guidry," I say to myself. "Without me who'd clean your toilets? It's my ma you married, and I'm part of the package come with her."

In addition to the portable toilets (each has on it a picture of a skunk and the name "Pepé Le Pew"), around back in the yard are trucks with 3,600- and 2,350-gallon tanks that say "WE'RE FULL OF IT" and "BE THERE IN A FLUSH." In Iberville and Assumption Parishes, people know my step-pa. His phone book ad reads:

"Mr. Biffy" Septic Tank Cleaning and Toilet Rental.
Call for Pricing/Specials for Parties, Weddings, Graduations,
Family Reunions, Construction Sites. Check Out Our Toilets at
The Fairgrounds. Remember "A Royal Flush Beats A Full House."

Working for hardly no wage, I am afflicted by shame. An outcast in his movies, Elvis also understands how it is feeling shamed and cursed. In *Flaming Star*, he is Pacer, a half-breed. In *Love Me Tender*, he is Vance's younger brother no one pays attention to till he marries Vance's girl when Vance is away at the Civil War.

This lady I know thinks I am as mixed-up as Danny Fisher—Elvis in *King Creole*, which takes place in New Orleans. She spells her name Bożena. She is one of them that arrived from Poland. We studied them in junior high. They are "Disgraced Persons." I like Bożena. She waits on tables. She's lots older but looks good in that pink uniform as tight as a hide.

My line of work doesn't embarrass me. She says I am in "toiletries." Though cargo slops back and forth in the tank, with my hair slicked back, no one mistakes me for Louie Guidry, which is the one thing I got over him the same as young Elvis playing Deke Rivers in *Loving You* has it over Wendell Corey, the older guy. On TV I've seen Elvis as Danny Fisher, Elvis as Deke Rivers, Elvis as Vince Everett in *Jailhouse Rock*. At the Gulf Star Theater, I have seen *G.I. Blues*, *Blue Hawaii*, *Spinout*, *Clambake*. It was something called a retroceptive look back at his great movies. Now Tom Dugas, stepson of Louie Guidry, plays the King of Rock 'n' Roll. My career spreads before me like the drainage field of a septic system.

Practicing the lip curl, I forget my lung, my nervousness. I forget L. Guidry who claims to have seen Elvis at the Louisiana Hayride in Shreveport. When I have said, "Tell me about Elvis," he's looked afar and replied, "If you'd mind your manners, I might-could tell you something about him." I know Guidry won't tell me a thing. It makes no difference to me when I'm rolling down the River Road, tank full of what Bożena calls "yoorine" as though it rhymes with the eye-care product. In some places as I drive, overhanging trees caress Guidry's truck the way I caress the Polish lady who makes me anxious saying it is a sin-sick world. Where it concerns sin, I'm a tight-wound spring. Despite his gospel singing with the Jordanaires, I believe Elvis to be a sinner. Though I have never performed it with a lady, I think the sin I want to know about is going to smell when we're done like the Dow Chemical in Donaldsonville, something you get used to.

A so-called Displaced Person, Bożena Iwanowski does not fit in here. Nor do I. People say I stink. She don't notice. Three times we've joyridden in the truck, last time when we pumped Simoneaux's tank. When I picked her up at the little room she rents, my looking at her chassis, her blonde hair, got me going. I wriggled about, curled my lip. "Rock a Hula. Let's go get us some toiletries," I had said March 11.

"What?"

"Just 'Rock a Hula, Baby.'"

I wanted to shake, rattle, and roll her, to dislocate my leg, throw out my hip. I bit down the right side of my teeth so she could see my jawbone clench. Trying to keep the lip under control, I stared into her eyes. "We gonna take a ride to Ducarnou's and Simoneaux's."

"Who are Szymonwicz and Ducarnowski?"

"It's customers," I told her.

"Can't we go to Smoke Bend where you live, Mr. Louie Guidry?"

"No Smoke Bend. No, ma'am," I said. "Can't do that."

I pulled off the road. We were two miles from her place in a rest area of shady pines. The windows were green from the pine pollen of March. She wiped her neck. Hot outside, I felt chilly from getting over pneumonia. She forced some of the tight waitress uniform between her legs. We were reading a sign: "NO TRESPASSING, hunting, fishing, gathering pecans, picking moss on Arcadia Plantation. Estate of George Mitchell."

"You need help out of your dress?"

"Not here can we do that," she said in her broken language of Polish. "I haf present for you. Open up the bag, Louie Guidry."

"My Lord! It's fuzzy dice," I said with excitement. They were better than Ma and Guidry give me for Christmas, birthday, graduation, when they don't usually present me but three pairs of work gloves.

The next place I pulled out of the evening heat she said, "You are only one for me." It was no place to stop in a septic cleaning and pumping truck. The sign under the pines read:

*No hunting or trespassing on any Ashland Chemical Property
located on the right descending bank of the Mississippi River*

approximately five miles below the City of Plaquemine,
Louisiana, and formerly known as the Oakwild and Herbert
Plantations.

"Where we are to go now? There is no place for us. I haf all my life felt there is nowhere for Bożena Iwanowski. I cannot return to Communist regime of Poland."

"Don't get down on yourself. What's the word 'regime' mean?"

"*Rezjim*, as I have pronounced it. *Rezjim*, government. You are only one left for me, Louie."

"That's all right, Mama," I said.

Pulling out of there, I slid the hem of her waitress skirt up her thigh. She was shook up when we passed the LSU Pecan Station. Her leg had chigger bites. She sat with it out of her skirt. When we got to Simoneaux's, pollen covered the windshield. Itching, I started the wiper blades going.

"Steal me," she said. Then said, "Do you hear somethink?"

"Bees," I said. I was almost self-pollinating. I snapped two fingers, bringing them close to my face the way Elvis does as if staring at a mystery in their rhythm. "Baby, I never did no wrong," I said. She was rubbing me. She was afraid Simoneaux saw her.

"He keeps bees," I said.

With pollen heavy inside, I had trouble breathing. All of a sudden, nervousness made me cough.

"I want to play house," she said.

"Where'd you learn to talk like that?" I asked as I jumped down from the truck cab.

I pulled out the hose. Working with the longest hose in the business, I pumped the tank.

The truck heavier by one hundred gallons of Simoneaux's waste, I got out of there, telling her I had business things to do, telling her next week (tonight!) I'll come get her at Skilley's Café and to have the fried chicken ready, telling her I am running a weeklong special for first-time customers—"After Three Pumps, Get Fourth Free." I didn't pump Ducarnou like "Mr. Biffy" Louie Guidry told me to.

During this last, long week, March 11–on, I have self-pollinated thirteen times thinking of Bożena. To hell with Guidry. I speed to her in the 2,350-gallon truck, which I'll return when I feel like it. The fried chicken and Skilley's Café's famous hush puppies await me. No road-side parking for us; we head to the Louisiane Motel with the greasy chicken boxes. As she pays for the room with her two weeks of tips, I shake a knee out of fear. To calm myself, I nibble a drumstick.

"Now I have a surprise," I tell her when we're inside.

At five of seven, we sit on the edge of the bed. Out of Baton Rouge comes a show on the TV about Elvis. After another piece of chicken, I comb my hair. Shoulder, knee, hip acting up, my voice gets lower. She has a beer. She looks at me, she looks at him. Curtains closed, we keep no lights on. TV flickers. People check into the motel, gab outside our window. It is an interview from his early days. On TV he wears a black suit, black shirt, white tie. Colonel Parker is behind him. "Elvis," reporters are asking, "some mothers and fathers think you're a bad influence on the young and that rock 'n' roll is harmful. What do you say?"

"Well, sir, ah-ah never wanted to, ah, do anything . . . to hurt anybody," he is saying. "No sir, ah-ah just wanna say to all the moms and dads of America that it's just good fun your sons and daughters are having. Ah, young teenagers have a lot of energy to burn off."

"You're telling me!" I say to him.

With the King there, Bożena blows on my face. I am trying not to pollinate. We are together in America, in Louisiana, U.S.A. Elvis is singing "Mystery Train" way back up on a stage in Birmingham or someplace when he first started out. She says his name. I say his name. The three of us are together. Me and Elvis. Elvis and Bożena. Bożena and me. When I jerk, she says, "Wait! You self-pollinated!" Confusing me with him, she says, "Elvis," then says, "You're a pollinator, Elvis! That's what you are, Mr. Self-Pollinator."

"No, I ain't, yes I am," I lie, then just as fast I tell her the truth about my sex life. I look away ashamed, see the King's shadow on the wall. "It's that I've been too long on Lonely Street."

"I haf, too, Louie," she says. "I haf lived there all my life until you come to Skilley's."

To show me how long she's been where the desk clerk's dressed in black, she begins a beautiful, strange song sounds like "O, mish-mash-something," but I can't say the foreign words. "Dreamer's Waltz," she says it means in Polish, then writes the first line on a slip of paper: "*O młynarce z pewnej wsi młody rybak ciągle śni.*"

She explains the song is about a miller's daughter. When the fisherman tells her he loves her, she thinks she is too good for him and leaves the village. When she comes back, the fisherman has someone new and tells her, "I'm sorry, your laugh is no good to me now."

"Elvis?" she says like I am her only hope. I look in her eyes. I see she really has no family, no Poland.

"Why you are not Elvis. You self-pollinated yourself, Louie. You haf made what is called 'premature—'"

"Inoculation," I say.

But she is wrong about prematurity, for hair slicked down, overall jacket collar up, I have a mystery train inside me sixteen coaches long. This could be Birmingham, this could be Memphis, this could be Crackow, Poland. With Guidry in Smoke Bend, I shake a shoulder, turn real slow. Lip curled high, I give her a hip move that gets her screaming in anticipation of my pollinating procedure. Flashbulbs popping, I yell to the Jordanaires, "Hit it, boys!" and give her the works.

When we are done (it has been the first time in my life), I say, "Bożena, you stung me."

"You stung me, Mr. Elvis Man."

"I guess we stung each other. I am grateful. I feel light-headed."

Both of us smarting from our stings, I think tonight on Lonely Street we won't be alone.

"And now we go to sleep, Louie," she says, singing softly again the words of sadness.

"No," I tell her. "Because of all kinda things, I can't sleep. Show's over. I have uresis. It's an embarrassment. Do you know what it is? I have a truck tank full of waste. I have worrisome problems as a businessman."

I know I will wet the bed if I stay with her. I will wet it good. Guidry will look for me. He will tell her who I am when he finds us.

"What other things you are worried over?" she asks.

"All kinda things," I say. "Bed wetting. Crying."

"They are not bad when we are together."

"No," I say. "I can't stay in this bed. It's bed-wetting, I tell you. Guidry calls me 'Sissy-Bed-Wetter' because of it."

"Who is this Guidry when you told me you are Guidry?"

"It's just my name," I tell her, covering up my mistake. "I'm Guidry, alias 'Mr. Biffy.' I have a split personality."

For sympathy, I pretend my bad lung is bothering me. "See?" I tell her. "See what happens when I get nervous?"

I bend over in the chair to show her how much the lung hurts. I cry out in terrible pain and anxiety, which starts her crying in sympathy. I cough like there is no tomorrow. She coughs, too. "I got pneumonia from portable toilets last winter. We have to go. I might wet myself. I'm sick, Bożena," I tell her, but I can't get her to move off the bed. She is crying for her Poland now, for us, for Elvis, for the Jordanaires, for Poland, for Buddy Holly, Little Richard, Gene Vincent, the Big Bopper, for Lithuania and Latvia, too. No one in any country has cried so hard. She tells me she has nocturnal uresis as well. She tells me every secret of her secret life. Bożena won't let me return to Lonely Street. "For us no more Lonely Street, Mr. Louie Guidry Elvis," she says and begins singing and coughing and singing to protect me from the pain of loneliness she herself has known all her life.

When she is doing the singing and coughing, she can't be hurt. Neither can I. Never in the world will we be hurt and lonely as long as we keep coughing and singing. I follow how she says it. "*O młynarce z pewnej wsi . . .*" After twenty times, I get the words right. I am singing in Polish. It's a mournful, happy song. Because of it, because of the song and the toiletries business, no one hurts us ever again, I think, until I hear brakes on the big truck screech, see the desk clerk dressed in black coming through the motel door, hear Mr. Biffy, my step-pa, behind him telling me to get home pronto and to quit coughing. "When you get back, air out that mattress you wet," he says, reaching for my nose, then grabbing my ear to pinch.

Singing the loneliness out of her heart and mine, Bożena with no Poland and no family is crying so hard I don't know what to do with Guidry squeezing my ear but let her hold on to the shirt cuff of my jumpsuit and admire me.

"*O młynarce z pewnej wsi,*" we sing.

THE LOW AUGUST FEVER

Behold the man Nelly flouncing about the lobby, misting the ferns, watering the potted palms. The more excited I am, the more exaggerated my movements. When the lady guest in 2C comes downstairs, I put a hand to my hip, crook an elbow, extend a ringed finger to my lips, and say excitedly, "Would you look at those earrings!"

Julian, the maintenance man, says, "You're so froufrou, Nelly."

"That means 'frilly ornamentation,' Julian."

"You know what it means," he says to irritate me. No matter what lies he makes up, I should calm myself so I can tell this from the start. "Take deep breath, exhale slowly," I say to myself. Now I'm ready for the tell-all.

Mr. Orville Lagro and the woman's wicked ways are the focus of this true confession as much as my own are. They were staying in Room 2C. For a couple of days, he'd been saying, "I bite myself where no one sees. I'm gonna bite and scratch myself to death. I can't stand being alone."

Before he'd hired her to bite and scratch him, the Polish lady in 2C told me she'd asked him over the phone, "Where is your home base? Do you have proper care (she meant 'car') insurance?"

"Yes, yes," said Mr. Lagro to her questions, directing her to call the owner of Hiram's General Goods, Ville Platte, Louisiana, if she needed references. Happily for her, when she called she was assured of the salesman's complete trustworthiness.

"I am Bożena then, Mr. Lagro," she said by way of introduction. "In the morning, I will meet you at filling station on the Pecan Street."

At this service station, she'd once dated an employee, Sonny, whose passion for good steaks had gotten him into trouble. She'd never get over him, she thought. Seeing Mr. Lagro stroll in as though he itched where he couldn't reach, she felt herself sinking deeper into hopelessness. She had to get away from Ville Platte, though. After Sonny, the grease monkey, had choked to death on a T-bone, she'd kept his suitcase. It was covered with decals: "Hot Springs Tonight," "Come with Me to the Sea of Love," "Be Mine," "Southern Serves the South," etc.

Over the days and nights we grew to trust each other, I, Nelly, studied the decals as she told me how, years before and eighty miles west of here, her father and brothers had cut sugarcane, shoveled bagasse, and done other things around the Del Rio Plantation, while her mother and she, Bożena, worked in the owner's house. His name was Pleasaunt. Because no one understood her when Bożena sang "*O Młynarce z Pewnej Wsi Walc*," her mother had to translate for them. Singing "Dreamer's Waltz" when she went into the canebrake with Mr. Pleasaunt, the young woman walking with the married man pretended she was in the old country. This was in 1949.

When the Iwanowskis moved north a few years later, she'd stayed at Del Rio. The cane grower had won her heart. She was twenty then, fifty now. With her makeup on, you'd never guess her age. We told each other everything. We told each other lies.

"Did he divorce his wife and marry you?" I asked.

"No," she said. She pulled out a crumpled letter where her mother called her "*Cygan*, Gypsy." "He put me on the Greyhound with what he called 'so long, good-bye pay.'"

After pining for him in Baton Rouge, Shreveport, Beaumont, and Marshall, where Bożena's heart still yearned for love years later, she met the grease monkey with the decal-covered suitcase. This is how she ended up in Ville Platte mourning Sonny's passing and waiting in a clean, white blouse for Orville P. Lagro.

Before I get too excited, let me say that Mr. Lagro began the lost nature talk I will soon describe, although Bożena, being far from her family all of her grown life, really has lost nature. Still, it was him, Lagro, who got *us* going on it. From Ville Platte, one yellowed fingernail scratching himself almost to death, bad luck and lost nature in the person of Orville Lagro drove an old Chevy south and changed our lives.

Now I will confess my secrets. Lost nature occurs when a person turns out different from what God intended him to be. I will tell you about my face powder. I will tell you I have a hairnet, the *poudre de riz*, and a silken dressing gown. I will also let you in on Orville Lagro's reproductive parts, his Slenderella waist cinch, his blond toupee. It will be worth the wait. You'll notice me get high-strung. Please let me say that people know the bishop would have allowed me to recover in the home for failed priests in Port Allen; but I had so disgraced the sacerdotal office that, in my mind, I could never be forgiven. After a few days of lobby talk at the Lafayette Inn guest house, Bożena and I understood we had lost natures as bad as anyone's. Consider me, for instance: I am a bug. A palmetto bug, I wait on the pavement of this French Quarter to be stepped on. This is how low I feel—bug low.

The fabric salesman Lagro, the émigré Bożena Iwanowski, the ex-cleric Nelly "Froufrou" Pontiff—each of us was troubled by the low fever that is August when we met in the lobby on the nineteenth of last month. Day in, day out, my parrot squawked, "I'm from Dixie. What's cookin', Cookie? This gumbo's cold, Nelly." Susceptible to crying jags, I wondered whether I could do right by the guests, Orville and Bożena, 'd ensconced in 2C overlooking the courtyard.

The first time I felt the rough touch of the salesman's hand, I thought e must itch something awful. As salesmen will, he kept his nails manicured, except the one on his right hand's little finger. The fingernail was an ugly yellow—long, sharp.

"I keep it sharpened, but only one so as not to scratch myself *too* much," he said. "You understand that some people just can't stand themselves."

"I like a long nail."

"Awk, whee-hoo," said Polly. "Long nail. Long nail."

In the courtyard the tile fountain gurgled. Bags in both my hands, another under my arm, I left the woman with her suitcase to carry, Lagro carrying nothing but the wig on his blond head and a loadful of self-hatred.

"When sir and madam go up, watch those stairs. I'll return with more fresh towels," I said as he handed me a tip and slammed the louvered door once they'd made it to the room.

"This isn't real hair growing. It's a blond-hair wig," he was saying. "Doubt you knew that being as how we just met three hours ago. I'm starting to itch. On the day I can step out of my body for the last time, I'll be fine. I'm self-allergicked. Even a twinge of conscience leads me to bite and scratch at the regret that comes from being Orville P. Lagro. My inner self rejects my outer self. Some people are allergicked to themselves when they have skin mites. My allergy sensitivity is for psychological reasons."

When the breeze stirred the banana plants and flames fluttered in the courtyard gas lamps, I slipped a preprinted card under their door: PREPARED TO SERVE YOU. SINCERE, SENSITIVE NELSON PONTIFF.

In the lobby, sniffling with self-pity, I regained my composure when I saw her staring through the office window. "Awk, whee-hoo, this gumbo's cold, Nelly," Polly was saying.

"Look, you're hurt," I said. "You've been scratched."

Calling her "Fair One," I handed her a Band-Aid from the desk. She gave me a sheet of paper. With a flourish of the wrist and a low bow, peeked at the note, the billet-doux, in which the salesman had written on Lafayette Inn stationery: "Confidential to Mr. Pontiff, Desk Clerk. I need assistance. I will gladly pay you. O. P. Lagro (Guest that checked in with foreign lady.)"

"I'm flattered," I said. Voice rising higher, I was giddy, yet I caught myself before telling her what he wrote.

When she left, I grabbed an armful of towels. With my ears to the door of Room 2C, The Gardenia Room, I heard him in there. "Self-hatred and punishment stemming from it is the way to improve my health," he was saying. "That's exactly why you've been hired, Missy Mae. Scratch me from here to H-E-double toothpicks, so I'll start healing. That's right, kindly bite me there, too."

Knowing I was eavesdropping, smirking Julian, the maintenance man, stepped around me on the second-floor gallery. Back down in the courtyard, Julian mimicked me, putting his hand to his ear as if listening to the gossip the hot wind caught. (When I'd interviewed him for the job in maintenance a year ago, I'd flinched during one part of it. "Oh, dear, didn't using something so big hurt him, Julian?" I'd asked. My feeling of superiority didn't last long despite my concern for what he'd done to his boyfriend's rectum.) When he crossed himself and pretended to pray, he made me want to cry. "Heard the gossip, Padre?" he called up.

"What is the parish saying about me?" I asked.

"You've been kicked out of the priesthood for all the shame you've brought it."

"Oh no, oh no! I feel faint." (This is a game we play.) I decided to stop by the Gardenia Room.

Holding back tears, I tapped on Mr. Lagro's door, said, "Towels?"

When the door opened, nails were scratching skin. "Holy Geez! More towels?" he was saying. "You got a fetish for them?"

"Thank you," Bożena said, her politeness releasing in me a flood of tears. Julian mocking me from the courtyard, I stumbled down the stairs again. "Oh, you're a beautiful mess," I sobbed when I saw my face in the mirror. "That kind lady's goodness, her concern for humanity, set against Julian's thoughtlessness make you weep."

Thankfully, evening fell as I powdered my face and shaved my legs.

When Julian isn't ridiculing me, when guests are enjoying themselves in the Quarter, I stroll the courtyard to recall my days of faith. I last did this August 21, when priests say the "Mass of a Holy Woman not a Martyr" in honor of St. Jane de Chantal, a Mass prescribed in the liturgical calendar. Thinking of Julian, of Polly the parrot, of my guest, I whispered, "The Lord be with you," before crossing Burgundy Street to my room in the annex to await Mr. Lagro's orders.

The next morning, his wig combed, his dark glasses on, here at nine o'clock he came through the lobby hefting two bags. Without a glance at the continental breakfast I'd put out, he left in the Chevy.

"Whoa," I said, "what was that in the billet-doux about needing my assistance?"

Still in a huff when I answered the phone, I said, "Yes, I know you don't need a mere desk clerk helping you. I don't know why you said you did."

It wasn't him calling. "I'm hungry," Bożena said.

"I'll bring you something."

After giving her employer a thorough scratching that morning, she was famished. Angry as I was at him, Bożena's having lunch without him made me tear up. "Guess your boss isn't calling today," I said when I phoned her later. "It's afternoon. No word from him. I guess he's punishing both of us now. What have I done to deserve it?"

We talked through the late afternoon. "How long are you staying?" I asked. "How long must the punishment last? Does he want me, Froufrou Nelly, to start itching?"

"We'f just begun our stay. I miss my love."

"Mr. Lagro?"

"No, Sonny Rachal. Six months ago, Sonny was cutting his steak. When he took a bite, open springed his eyes. I hit his back while he thumped his chest. He was choking, his eyes were watering."

"Dear you, dear, dear you for suffering so much, Bożena."

"It was emergency. The steak was hot, Sonny was cold. 'Well,' said the police cops when they got there, 'looks like he's history, but a steak is a steak,' and they sat down and requested his favorite steak sauce. There is my dead Sonny, and they are eating his T-bone."

"The message I hear is one of sadness. What comforts a person at such times? What words to comfort you?"

"I don't know where Mr. Lagro is," she said. "He has left money for me to wait here."

On August twenty-fourth, letters and postcards arrived for Orville Lagro from Orville Lagro. After beginning "Mr. Wrecker-of-a-Life," one postcard read, "You've never been happy wi'f your soul. Signed: Orville (Your Outer Skin)."

Soon after, she began fretting he'd been scratched away from her, had maybe paid someone else to do her job, which would leave her unemployed. Careful not to let on what I'd learned eavesdropping, I asked, "What was in his sample case I carried up for him?"

"Fabrics. I am a displaced person."

"Looks like so is he. He hasn't been back," I said, wondering how she could care for someone so self-allergicked as Orville Lagro.

"Whee-hoo, I'm from Dixie. Hi ya, Cookie. Let's have a drink some-time," Polly said to her.

If I interpreted Polly's "whee-hoo" correctly, she was telling me Bożena was a tough cookie who'd endured the steak-choking death of a good man. Bożena was worn down at fifty like the crazy men wear-ing miniskirts and makeup on Bourbon Street; like the drunks fight-ing on the levee by the brewery; like the nervous, anxious Nelly-priest, Froufrou Nelly, unable to control his venery while the bishop insisted he control it. Worse for Bożena, she had just lost her mother and come back south to live without a family.

In the world of entomology will be found lost nature. Bożena lies dying on Dumaine Street. A breath of air moves her blue butterfly wings. A lonely palmetto bug, I lie waiting between the bricks of the courtyard. Waiting for what? My antennae stir in the touch of air that moves the butterfly's dead wings. To think like this makes one wonder: aren't we all tired of the heat? *Go home to the North. Go home, old, beautiful, blue-winged butterfly. Allez vous-ens, dear, sensitive Bożena.*

I don't know if she can. Once a person's nature has fled (this I tell you from experience), the person too often lacks strength to experiment and trick the nature back into working order—all except Orville Lagro. That's the password: Orv Lagro–Lost Nature. Lost Nature–Orv Lagro. I see those afflicted with it wandering about. Seeing them in an alley, I whisper, "Is it lost nature with you, lad?"

"Yessir, lost nature here," they'll say.

"It's terrible to try to escape it alone. Let me help."

Sometimes, in the midnight shadows of Decatur Street, we find ourselves in each other's arms. In that moment, in that room, we are no longer lost—till dawn comes like the river. Then shadows vanish, true natures vanish, like Mr. Lagro from himself. Lost Nature. Orville Lagro. Password.

The day before we celebrate the Beheading of John the Baptist in the Catholic Church, Mr. Lagro sent instructions to find him. En route, I stopped at Maison Blanche to admire the linen jackets in the window. A young man fresh from a workout at the New Orleans Athletic Club said, touching my elbow, "You all right? On the way to lift weights? Do you have lost nature? My name is Etienne."

"I'm going to the Fairmont Hotel. Don't mind my tears." Clutching his arm, I pretended to be faint. "Lilac water splashed about my temples would revive me," I told him. The August heat brings memories that make me light-headed. My church was in St. John the Baptist Parish. On the eve of that saint's beheading, realizing it's a hard time of year for me, Julian gave me an umbrella to shade me from the sun. As sweet Etienne escorted me to the Fairmont Hotel, he carried the umbrella. Just as I was drying my tears, closing the thing with its torn cloth and splayed ribs, and bidding adieu to the youthful muscle man, a fantastically blond, pompadoured figure named Orville Lagro appeared in the pillared lobby of the hotel.

"How I look?" he asked. Mr. Lost Nature appeared healthier than at the guest house where he'd occupied the Gardenia Room, 2C. Without the constant scratching, his skin had been rejuvenating.

"Forgive my impertinence, dear sir, but who shaved your eyebrows? They're bare."

"I give a barber a dollar. The rest of me I shaved myself," he said. "Yessirree, Orville is mending. No more scratching away shame when I'm done with myself. Praise Jesus. Do you want to come upstairs? I got a room here. Let's have a drink. I bet your parrot says that when he wants to meet a lady."

"I'm lonely. I'll be flattered to join you."

"I don't mean for nothing funny. You're about to see the last of Orville Lagro."

"What do you mean?"

"I mean let's have a Sazerac in the bar."

"Please to make mine a Ramos Gin Fizz," I told the bartender, which is the Fairmont's famous drink.

"You still a little sissy always fussing for his bottle? I guess I understand. I've got plenty reason to cry and fuss. You want to meet someone."

"I like meeting people. I'll taste my gin fizz right now. Do you know what day is tomorrow, August 29, in our church? Forgive me if I lose emotional control."

"Whatever it is, we're moving it up to today," he said. "This yours?"

he asked about the umbrella. "I didn't think it was raining. You remember the two-dollar tip I give you when me and the Polish lady pulled in from Ville Platte—you carried our bags up? One bag was my salesman's sample case."

"Fine fabrics are in it, you told Bożena."

"That tip you got back then was nothing compared to what you're gonna see. Take your gin fizzy. Grab the umbrella. Let's meet my partner. You know the problem was that led to my scratching?" he asked on the way up in the elevator. "It was unreliability. That's the sole secret. Plus I'm a low-grade liar. For instance, you know the fine fabrics I sell?" (We were in the room.) "Look in that case of samples. No, don't look. Close your eyes, rub your hands on what's inside."

"A rather too coarse texture that's not silky."

"It's your circular-type, towel dispenser–type cloth for use in gas station, café, or nightclub men's rooms. It's the on'y fine fabric I ever sold. See about my lying?"

"So you fib. That's no reason for your skin to itch. I mean look at me, an ex-priest. The bishop told me, 'Seek help for your habit, Nervous Nelly.' I disobeyed. I kept practicing it. Nervous Nelly is a slave to passion. Why do you think my room in the annex is notorious in the French Quarter? Men of all sizes visit. This is my penance. August is my penance. The *Quartier Français* is my penance."

"See, you do too have an itch, Pastor. Mine acts different from yours. I've almos' scratched myself out of existence. Unreliable in marriage, jobs, w'if my kids, w'if money, w'if alcohol and gambling. Been scratching leading up to this week. Now I got that little ol' Polish gal with none to count on but me. You know she's a 'Disgraced Person,' who's asked me to give her a permanent place, but I can't. If I took her along in my life, she could never rely on Orville Lagro. Henceforth, I'm not myself so no one should rely on me. Watch close. There ain't going to be no Orville Lagro ever again."

Turning over the sample case, he let the cloth towels he sold tumble to the floor. "I'll th'ow these items in here in the empty sample case—old sunglasses, deodorant, aftershave lotion. All this stuff I'm th'owing out. See?" he said next, finger pointing to his eyebrows, "no hair." When he took off his shirt, he pointed to his chest, then lifting his arms, pointed there. "Not a lick of it. Hairless as a whistle. Shaved clean. Hair and all, I now leave Orville Lagro behind me. Au revoir."

Before I could say "What's cookin', Cookie?" he was buck naked except for the blond wig, which he was yanking at, curling it up at the sides until it flew off with a pop, and I cried, "The Beheading of John the Baptist a day early," and fell to my knees where I found myself face to face with parts more hairless than his head.

"You ask at the desk for Orville P. Lagro, and there's no such a one registered. Reach over there. Th'ow me that set of underpanties. Currently residing in this suite of rooms is one Mr. C. L. Sloboda, a wheat grower from the outskirts of Dickinson. That's right—Dickinson in the Peace Garden State. Please excuse while I visit the bathroom. Say," he said from in there, "you know why I tease you? Because maybe I'm a pansified sissy who's ashamed of things of that nature I did in my past."

I heard him shuffle around breathing heavily until, in a second, open swung the door and out walked a brown-haired, handsome man in white shirt and powder blue slacks. It looked like the man had squeezed himself into the Slenderella waist cinch I'd seen on the bed. Where, I wondered, has Mr. Lagro gone? The "business partner" had on no eyeglasses, was wearing a different aftershave lotion. His scent filled the room. "There's something about an Aqua Velva man. I'm Chet Sloboda," he said. He extended a firm, dry hand, then adjusted the brown wig. "Here's your tip in the envelope plus directions for when I stop at the Lafayette to see am I recognized by a sad Polish lady. This ol' sample case from my haunted past, you just th'ow it in the river."

Confident, well-dressed, he was tricking himself out of lost nature. The long fingernail was gone. "First time in New Orleans for Chet Sloboda, loyal son of North Dakota. Is there someplace around here to eat?" he said, dropping his voice.

"Try the Oysters Bienville at Felix's," I said, making the sign of the cross as I hurried away from him.

Wig, shirt, "underpanties," as he called them, sticking out of it, I gave the samples case to a panhandler on Orleans Street. Perplexed by witnessing someone besides myself, with my face powder, my hairnet, my kimono, my high heels, become someone new, I hurried back. Addressed to Orville Lagro, a postcard awaited me at the Lafayette. No return address, no other name on it but his, a plain, white postcard that read: "It is done and over with."

To Bożena, I said nothing about the drink Mr. Lagro called a "gin fizzy," nothing about his hairless reproductive parts and about my visitation with him.

She waited, she fretted. When he came back, she was in the courtyard listening to Julian. He'd been to the library to look up information about the Louisiana Resettlement Program. "There were 1,044 displaced persons here in 1949 and '50. Girly was one of them. In sugarcane country, some complained of harsh treatment," Julian was saying as Mr. Lagro edged out of sight behind a palm frond.

It wasn't fair that Orville Lagro, Orville Sloboda— . . . I mean Chet Sloboda of Dickinson, didn't give her a good look at himself while Julian rambled on. Listening to Julian, she'd glanced over—that was it, a single glance! With all of his changes, she probably wouldn't have recognized him anyway. Mr. Sloboda aka Lagro was conducting a test to see whether his old lost nature could be discerned under the new-nature disguise. I'd been paid ten dollars to keep quiet about who'd come in wearing Aqua Velva and a waist cinch. Even Polly must've thought Chet Sloboda was a tourist asking directions to Audubon

Park. Chet Sloboda played the part, asking whether I'd heard anything about today's grain futures and saying New Orleans was a pretty place, but it wasn't North Dakota. After a while, he whispered, "Thanks. She don't recognize me."

"Flattered to assist," I said, as Mr. Sloboda, even better-natured than three days before in the Fairmont Hotel, escaped out the door.

Bożena (myself, too, I confess) had looked forward to his mail. What fun waiting for the postman. In the days before payment for his room ran out, she longed for Mr. Lagro to write cards to himself. "I desire to take care of my employers," she said when our chitchat was done. "Where is he wandering tonight and today?" (Was she thinking of her sweet time on a Plaquemine sugar plantation? Was she thinking of Mr. Pleasaunt from so many years ago? Was she thinking of Mr. Lagro, who was displaced more than either of us, but now was a new person named Chet Sloboda?)

"Why didn't you ever go north?" I asked as Julian rambled on about the governor establishing a state commission on DPs to deal with the problem in Louisiana.

She never answered straight except to say she was a sinner who'd embarrassed her family. "I only just got back from there."

"The Lord forgives you," I told her.

"Why you are then so displaced yourself, Mr. Desk Clerk?" she asked.

"Because I can't forgive myself. I never forget my history, my shame- ul nights when I would entertain in the rectory. I'm not what I could ›e. Can't you see how frantic I am? How uncontrollably accommo- lating? My voice is rising. I'm getting shrill. I have to control myself. ulian, the hairnet! The *poudre de riz*! Will you get them please, Julian? ✓ly lost nature has returned."

"Heard the gossip, Nelly?" asked Julian, upsetting me more by fold- ng his hands in prayer and pursing his lips.

"What were people saying about me? Were they saying I've left the priesthood? Were they saying I wear lipstick?"

Julian managed to calm me, the dear. After this latest flare-up, there is no gossip to report. He helped me powder my face. He helped me with my kimono. He told me the DPs who'd had complaints about life on the sugarcane plantations were sent north. Our waiting for Mr. Lagro, I in my kimono and high heels, grew dull. With nothing to talk about once I'd confessed to her that I snooped in guests' rooms and hated loving Julian, I trained Polly to say five new words, not counting the "whee-hoos." If someone asks the way to Perdido Street, Poll says, "You're here. This is hell. Whee-hoo! Whee-hoo!" That's when I chime in, "Will good sir need a room tonight in the annex?"

September comes in with my training Polly and with Bożena forced to seek employment. Bożena and I pray the Litany of the Saints before she goes looking for night work. "Lord have mercy . . . Christ have mercy," we say over and over. Counting our blessings, our voices drone on into the twilight. "Though some people can't leave their past, some are darn sick of traveling around in it," Orville Lagro would say. Łomza, Poland; Plaquemine and Donaldsonville, Louisiana; Marshall, Texas; Ville Platte. She's been one heck of a traveler. A courtyard can be a restful place to such a person with decals on her suitcase. A room in an annex is better than no room at all. "Lord have mercy," Bożena and I say in unison. Polly joins us. Fancy, a praying parrot! My credibility is important, so I will tell you (not as gossip, dear me no, but as straight fact) that on *Rue* Toulouse, which crosses Burgundy, Bożena stood for a week as black shells under the streetlamp passed at a crawl. If the car stopped and the drivers had money, she joined them for a ride.

Have you heard it said, "There is no place hotter than a New Orleans kitchen in August?" Change the month to September. Make it September 16, and, tired of her night job, you will find Bożena slave away now in the kitchen of a third-rate restaurant on St. Peter Street

She's back to the kind of work she did at Howdy, Pardner in Marshall, Texas, or at Skilley's in Donaldsonville, Louisiana. Wouldn't it be funny if Pleasaunt, the sugarcane grower from years ago, came in while she was waitressing? Wouldn't it be the most delicious gossip if Mr. Chet Sloboda in a brown wig and waist cinch stopped in for étouffée? Displaced, disoriented, Bożena falls into bed across the street in the room next to mine after asking me if there's been mail from a fabric salesman. When I shake my head no, we both weep in such jags and fits as you will never see, while all this time—*all* this time, mind you, which really saddens me—lucky Mr. Sloboda is walking around New Orleans with a new identity and skin that glows.

THE WAND OF YOUTH

When the bus from Peter Cooper Orthopedic School drops them off, Francis, this sixteen-year-old neighborhood kid and my sister's friend, escorts her to our back porch, bows to her like a count or nobleman, then hobbles home on crutches with hard, leather cuffs that circle his forearms. Because Francis is politer than anybody needs to be, my friends call him "the Noble Pole."

When we're playing basketball and he wants to join us, he leans his crutches against the garage, stands at the free throw line we draw in the alley, and yells stupid things like "Hustle him! Hustle him!"

"You're not being polite, Francis," Lesczyk Iwanowski and I remind him.

"Hustle him, please," he corrects himself.

He can't turn without crutches. If he's not facing the basket, he can't shoot. Stealing the ball from him is easy though he has strong arms and is older than us.

Last February, these seventeen-year-olds kidnapped him. They paid a fellow to buy them beer in the county where it's legal to drink at eighteen. Francis had three cans of Grain Belt. With the six-packs gone, they drove Bill Nicoski's dad's car to Allouez Sauna in the neighborhood across the Left-Handed River from the East End, my neighborhood. In a country of Finns, it's not unusual for young or old—Finnish, Swedish, or Polish—to go to a steam bath or sauna after drinking. Francis's stiltlike legs don't bend. Because of this, he's always made a big deal out of no one seeing them, which would have happened if he'd taken off his clothes. Who knows what names the guys would call him once they saw his legs? If he didn't join them, he'd have to walk home in the bitter cold.

When they got the sauna to one hundred and seventy degrees and were wondering if he'd left or was still out in the changing room, in walked Francis in long underwear. Who wears long underwear? The guys start to laugh. In a minute, the underwear is soaking wet and Francis is passed out, but he's preserved his legs as a mystery no one will see. One of the great secrets of East End, along with why does Peewee Jablonski talk to the jukebox on Trinity Sunday, is What do Francis's legs look like?

Edie Juncewicz, my sister Janina's other friend besides Francis, attends school with me, or she did until she graduated ahead of me. Watching us through her thick glasses, she tells us we have something that one day will be lost to us. "The wand of youth is precious," she says, waving her hands as though she holds this wand. Though Edie frowns when classmates tell jokes, she smiles when the nuns call tennis shoes "tennis slippers" or boxing gloves "killer mittens." She does this to please them. The wand of youth has passed her by. A teenager and an old woman rolled into one, she cries over my sister and the map of Poland.

Nowadays, in 1954, East End ladies collect money for polio research March of Dimes donation cans stand in all of the stores, and my sister prays nearly nonstop she will be healed. After she returns from the Orthopedic School with the Noble Pole, she prays hard enough that Lesczyk Iwanowski's mother can hear her. This gets Mrs. Iwanowski going next door, so that we hear her in Polish praying for what I do not know. For centuries, the Black Madonna of Częstochowa, a blessed icon, has guarded Polish people, Polish homes, Polish armies. I think Mrs. Iwanowski's prayers are going unanswered because she has a daughter who never comes home to see her. Janina's prayers, too, seem to go unanswered because in this family, Dad is stuck in a job on the packing floor at the flour mill, Janina is crippled, and Ma herself can't do a thing but listen to Chopin on the phonograph and pray into the evening. All I do is write and write about it all.

Thankfully, unlike my sister, I have normal friends. Mrs. Iwanowski's son is one of them. His family came from the old country. Lesczyk takes my mind off of how people treat my sister as though she is special and how she has two weird friends—although the neighbors think Lesczyk is weird for drawing pictures of birds and flowers like he is possessed by them. He has drawn wild lupines, European bellflowers, and the wood violet, the state flower of Wisconsin. He has drawn the white eagle that is the symbol of Poland. In blue chalk all over the neighborhood, you see it on walls, sidewalks, even on the cement foundation of the railroad switching station that has been torn down on Ninth Street. When it washes away, other kids redraw the eagle.

"Why'd the nuns keep you?" Mother asks me when I return from helping the Sisters pack schoolbooks for the summer. It is Memorial Day.

"That's how they are. They have nothing else to do, Ma," I say. In preparation for the 11 a.m. Memorial Day service at the cemetery, I salute her and head back outside. "Sister Benitia told me I'm going to be passed to the next grade, by the way. She said it was close, but that I finished the makeup work."

She's distracted by Janina and doesn't worry about me. A man with mission, I can take care of myself. I will get through Memorial Day. I will finish high school. I will graduate and work on an ore boat sailing from here to Buffalo. Joe and Margaret's son, Janina's brother. I read and write all the time of my observations of the East End.

Usually not much is going on around here to write about, but today, walking down Fourth, I see people planting flowers, cutting the grass, straightening the flags that fly on porches. It being the first hot day of spring, the elm trees leaf out. The air smells like lilacs and aspen trees. Everything blooms, and I am finished with school for three months.

When I turn toward Ninth Street, I see the cars by the cemetery. You can't find a place to park around here. Late arrivals must hurry, which is not easy, for some of them are so old they've lost relatives in the Spanish-American War. At a gravestone that says WHAT THE HEART HAS OWNED AND HAD, IT NEVER LOSES, Mr. Ham leans on his cane. He is president of the Polish Club. He has the Club's wreath with him. Because he gives part of his pension to the church, he's known in East End as "Good Ham, *Dobrze Szynka*." Certain old ladies have another name for him. Mrs. Snadiak calls him "*Glista*" ("worm" in Polish) because he drinks so much, which he does because his legs get what he calls "phanthom" pains. He wears support stockings made of thick, skin-colored cloth like my Grandma Fronckiewicz wears. Today he has on dressy, tan-colored lady's gloves.

"Why you wearing the gloves, too?" I ask.

"Helps my arthritis."

Because of his pain all over, it is hard for him to walk without stopping to lean on something. When I think about my sister, about Francis Zukowski, about Mr. Ham, and about the trouble the three people have walking, I want to make sure my legs work.

"*Czekać!* Wait!" Mr. Ham calls when I go too far from him toward the monument where people are congregating.

Standing on the platform, Father Tracy, speaking into a microphone, asks everyone to bow their heads in remembrance of Memorial Day. Mr. Ham edges me forward. Holding the wreath he's brought in the car, he limps a little toward the Moose Club, Elks Club, and the Woodmen of the World. Good Ham wears a blue work shirt with military ribbons hanging from the front. These honorable men have on white shirts, some with ties. Compared to the Polish Club wreath carry, organizations like the United Commercial Travelers have beautiful, twenty-five-dollar wreaths with red and yellow roses, chrysanthemums, white carnations. The line of wreaths stretches a half block back toward the NP ore dock.

The Polish Club's wreath, which represents the old-timers including my dad and grandpa in the neighborhood—and many who live elsewhere in Superior—is built of three hard wires forming a crooked A. Leaves and vines no one has dusted during the year hang from it. Plastic daisies peek out from plastic greenery. Plastic ivy dangles in back. The wire frame is four feet high, the wreath three feet around. A wrinkled streamer reads, THADDEUS KOSCIUSZKO CLUB OF SUPERIOR.

Thinking no one sees him, which is impossible with this many people here, Mr. Ham breaks out a pint bottle that says Peach-something on it.

"Woodmen of the World, march forward," a VFW official announces over the microphone when the blessing is over. I get nervous thinking about passing through the two rows of people that form an aisle. After his drink, Mr. Ham seems calm. Seven groups are called before we are. "Front and center. Place your wreath, Polish Club."

Memorial Day honors the war dead, not war veterans, but when we march up, I think of my uncles Walt Ostrowski, wounded on Iwo Jima, and Augie Fronckiewicz, who fought in Belgium. No matter what Mr. Ham looks like in a work shirt, nor how funny looking the wreath, our people are as important as anyone's. As I march beside Mr. Ham, my heart sinks with sorrow for the lost. Pushing the ends of the wire frame into the earth, we salute the flag and the wreath. We salute Father Tracy, the minister from Pilgrim Lutheran, and the rabbi from the temple, then we do an about-face.

At the solemn moment when a club's representatives are marching back through the crowd, nobody is supposed to talk. Now ladies are putting handkerchiefs to their mouths. Men are lowering their heads. When Mr. Ham starts saying, "By golly, we have a bright future with the Polish youths like you involved in the Polish Club," I think they are trying not to laugh. Probably relieved that we are done, he takes another nip from his bottle and slips a dollar into my shirt pocket.

"What are you drinking, Mr. Ham?" I ask.

"Orange pop," he says.

When he loses his balance, people laugh out loud. I bet he has been at the Warsaw Tavern since eight in the morning. He is complaining about phanthom pains and galloping pains. "By golly, they hurt," he says to people as he passes. "The stiffness is from being so patriotic," he says. "After the Italian-Americans, more Polish boys from the U.S. served in World War II than from any et'nic group. Get your sister a present, Tadek. Here's a dollar. She's in your house all-a-time."

"You gave me a dollar already, Mr. Ham."

"By golly, take another one for her present."

"Thank you," I say. But he is not done. Stumbling to pick up the daisies that have fallen from the wreath, he hands them and the wreath to me for safekeeping. "You take it home. Tell your dad to look after it until next year." During "Taps" he looks like he is crying. I have heard what Mr. Ham and his brother went through on D-Day.

When I walk home after the service, wearing the wreath around my shoulders and carrying the wire frame in one hand, I think I have done the Club proud by taking over for veterans who've had to work today, Polish East Enders—Ed Novack, Walt Simzek, Tony Stromko, my dad Joe Ostrowski. On and on goes the list of these veterans. Mr. Ham is on it somewhere, phanthom pains and all.

"Don't slouch. Walk straight," he says when he drives past on Fifth Street. "You represent the Club now." In his hand is the bottle of peach schnapps. I do as he says. Straightening my posture, I make sure anyone coming past will be able to read the THADDEUS KOSCIUSZKO streamer.

While I've been out, Mother has put lilacs in a vase on the kitchen table. I hear her tell someone Janina is resting. I hear Ma call from the hallway, "Edie and Francis to see you."

"Okay, Ma," my sister answers.

After ten minutes, it dawns on the visitors she's not coming down. Their faces sink.

"We'll be back later," Edie says. She and Francis leave for wherever people like them go. Edie calls my mother "*Pani* Ostrowska" on the way out.

"How was it today?" Mother asks when they leave. She's heard about Mr. Ham already. She has a name for him: "*Dupa* . . . ass."

"Fine, everything went fine," I tell her, but I'm not sure about a ceremony that can ever honor the dead enough or that she is right about Mr. Ham. So what if he is trying to get over what happened to him on D-Day?

After lunch, I get bored hanging around. In the East End, everything is closed except the taverns. Peering through the window of the Warsaw, I see Mr. Ham in his gloves enjoying a bowl of beer. On the accordion, some lady is playing "The White Cliffs of Dover." I salute *Dobrze Szynka*, who deserves my respect, which extends to my dad and all the others who served in wartime, Polish Club members or not.

From here, I go to Stanski's Market and Kashuba's Clothing Store. "Closed for Memorial Day," read signs in the windows. With nothing else to do, I think of visiting Francis Zukowski but am afraid he will bow to me and want to be polite.

If I am polite, perhaps my neighbor will have something for me to do. At her house, I ask to look through the magazines she stores in her shed. To keep out the rain and wind, Mrs. Iwanowski tacks magazine covers and newspapers to the wall. The Iwanowskis came to America under the Displaced Persons Act of 1948. They know about war. Right now, Lesczyk and her other boys are working on a Polish man's farm in Pierz, Minnesota.

"If you sweep and t'row t'ings out of shed, Tadek, I give you money," Mrs. Iwanowski says. She has asked me to do this before. Without her sons, she counts on me. On the dirt floor of the rickety shed, *Life*, *Look*, and *National Geographic* are stacked with the Polish newspapers. A neighborhood kid sweeps leftover wheat from empty boxcars in the railyard for her to feed her chickens.

When I am through stacking things and sweeping up, I sit on the back stoop of our house to look through a *Coronet* magazine. A dime richer for my payment from her, a dollar richer from the Mr. Ham payout, if I call up to my sister to tell her I have a dollar for her, too, Janina won't believe me, not since I once told her that Jesus was on our back porch looking for her and saying that she was beautiful.

I am thinking how last week Ma picked wild roses for her from the Iwanowskis' field. The fragrance clung to Mother's hands. Placing a bowl of water with a rose in it on the mantelpiece, Mother gave a wild rose to Janina. When Janina proceeded toward the Black Madonna's picture, Ma held her arm. The Polish Madonna has scars where Swedish invaders slashed Her face on the portrait that hangs in Jasna Góra. The Madonna cradles Jesus, a child, in Her arms. His two fingers are raised in blessing as though He holds the wand of youth. With my sister praying, I knew the Madonna would heal her regardless of what Dad says privately about her chances.

Two dollars and ten cents wealthier on the afternoon of my last day at *Skoła Wojciecha*, St. Adalbert's School, I bring the Polish Club wreath upstairs to Janina's room. She watches as I set the wire frame next to her bed, place the wreath on it. Propped against a pillow, she sits on her blue quilt. She is delicate. Her arms and wrists look fragile compared to mine. A breeze pushes the window shade inward. Sunlight brightens the bed, then the breeze pulls the shade back. She has combed her light brown hair. It falls to her shoulders. Looking as though she's going on a date, she sits alone in a dress with a white collar. She has leg braces on.

"You know what I did, Janina?"

"What?"

"I represented the Polish Club at the cemetery. I bought you some thing." As I place the daisies on her bed, I say, "I didn't buy these. They're a memento that fell off of the wreath. They're plastic. Here's a dollar from Mr. Ham."

The breeze moving the shade, I go to my room for the other present. When I return, my sister says, "Weren't the stores closed? Where could you buy a magazine? Nothing's open today."

"I got it with a dollar," I tell her, never thinking she'd know the stores were closed.

She's twirling the daisies in her hands. "You couldn't have bought it."

"I suppose it came from outer space. It's too bad if you don't trust me," I say. "Where do you think it's from?"

"All I said is you didn't buy it."

"How do you know when you're stuck in here all day?"

She can't say anything back to this.

Outside, I fiddle with the strings holding the clematis vine to the trellis below her window. I can hear the music from Janina's radio coming through the window screen. I'm disappointed in her for not believing me.

When I go next door, Mrs. Iwanowski says I can keep the magazine. "The Future Looks Better for Disabled Veterans," it says on the front, but it's two years old. Janina must have seen the date. I think of all the other things she knows about me from Edie and Francis. Now I could add this embarrassment with the *Coronet* magazine.

Seeing how stupid I am, I tell Mrs. Iwanowski I worked all morning for the nuns, that I brought my sister the magazine. I'm talking so fast I don't know what I'm saying. "I don't think I'm cut out to be Polish," I say to her.

I think she misses her sons, who might have done the same thing to their sister if she wasn't living far away in Louisiana. Drying her hands on her apron, she says something in Polish. She smiles at me as though she's traveled a very long distance, maybe from Częstochowa in Poland where the Madonna is, and that in her travels she has seen everything. Unsure of what to do, I salute her, *Pani* Iwanowski, the way I saluted the wreath at the cemetery, then I head off through the fields that make up so much of Superior. I could walk through them forever thinking about my sister Janina. A year older than me, she is too serious. She's gotten ill, and we don't know what to do about it. Brother and sister. If I say the words in Polish, they will haunt me. I wish Lesczyk was here. Even Francis Zukowski wouldn't be bad to have around. I'd apologize for when those guys made him drink the Grain Belt beers. If I acted more like the Noble Pole, especially toward my sister, I would be better off.

I don't know why I collect handfuls of the tall grass that blooms in the meadow above the river. White and yellow clover grows here. Absentmindedly, I collect the present for Janina, and when I have a bundle of grass, I think it is time to head back to her.

"What's she talking about that you gave her a wreath, Tadek?" Mother asks when I come in.

"I brought the Polish Club wreath up there," I say.

"That old thing?" Mother asks.

She is listening to a Paderewski recording on the phonograph. Except for the dim light from my grandmother's lamp in one corner, the room is dark with the quiet beauty of a warm May evening. When I bend to kiss Mother, she says, "*Kto prędko daje, dwa razy daje* . . . He who gives freely gives twice.'"

Upstairs, everything is quiet except for the phonograph music drifting up here. Paderewski is a Polish composer and statesman. After a while, I hear the hum of engines at the flour mill where Dad works from three to eleven. I hear a tug on the bay signal to an ore freighter headed for East Chicago or a grain boat for Buffalo—but in the next room, no sound.

Once in bed, I hear my sister. I think she is saying, "What kind of brother are you, Tadek?"

"If it helps you, I will listen to you say whatever you want about me," I tell her, ashamed to go in to see her. Over and over she is saying, "What kind of brother was I given?" then saying it in Polish, and I am whispering, "With this wand of youth, I will make it up to you, Janina."

When I bring her the bundle of grass, I lay it at the foot of her bed gently and kiss her hand. I do not know what I want it to mean. Perhaps the long grass will turn into straw we can use for Jesus' manger later in the year. I say nothing.

At nine-thirty when Dad comes home, the little I've done for my sister is as quiet as my whispers. As I listen to Janina, I begin praying to the patron saint of Poland. I am certain St. Adalbert will hear my prayers. He has heard them before. There is so much to request with prayers and a wand of youth—a better job for Dad, a life less worrisome for Mother, a new wreath for the Polish Club. Mostly tonight my prayers to St. Adalbert concern Janina.

At ten o'clock, I hear Dad in the next room saying he works hard for us. "I'm proud of your brother for how he helped *Dobrze Szynka*. At the tavern, I heard all about it. I'm proud of you for keeping your chin up. You don't give in, I don't give in," he says to my sister.

When he comes into my room, he asks, "Are you up?" From inhaling so much flour dust at work, he has a hard time catching his breath. After stopping at the Warsaw Tavern, he's had a beer in the kitchen. He doesn't do this often, but today is Memorial Day.

"I can't sleep," I tell him.

"I'm proud of you for everything," he says. "I keep thinking how 'From a good nest come good children.' Don't let nobody tell you it isn't important to be Polish."

When he carries in the Polish Club wreath, I see that my sister has wound the grass in such a way as to hold on the daisies to make them and the ivy on the wreath look real.

"I've decided to be president of the Club someday," I tell him.

"*Bardzo dobrze*, very good," he says laughing as he pats the top of my head. "Should we leave the wreath up here for tonight, Mr. President?" he asks. "Maybe we should start you as sergeant at arms. You can protect the wreath."

"Yes," I say in Polish as he stands it in the corner by the closet where, covered in cloth bags, his old army uniforms hang.

By now, Mother, who I haven't paid attention to all day but should have, is coming upstairs to the room across the hall. Halfway up, I hear her say, "Oh dear," and turn around. "If I put on another phonograph record, Chopin this time, the machine will shut off automatically when it's through playing, won't it, Janusz?" she calls to my dad.

"Yes," he says. Since my sister's gotten sick, Mother needs reassurance about everything.

With the windows downstairs open, the house smells like lilacs. You can hear the Chopin record Mother has started to play, though not as clearly as if you were with her in the moonlit living room downstairs, where she has gone again to kiss the Child in the Madonna's arms until Dad comes to rescue her.

"Come upstairs, Agnes," I hear him saying, coaxing her.

"I love Chopin. I'm not tired yet."

"Come. The Madonna will be here to kiss tomorrow, just as Poland will be. Chopin and Paderewski as well."

"Her Child with Her? I want Her Child to be with Her."

"Yes," says my father. "Her Child will be with Her. We have good children, too, you know. Let the phonograph shut off by itself now, and you can listen for a while in the moonlight upstairs."

ONE RED ROSE
ON A NEW BLACK DRESS

Except for the ore carrier *Joseph C. Wilson*, there is nothing down there on the bay but the windswept pier pushing out a half mile into the harbor ice. East of the pier lies Hog Island, where no one lives. West is the flour mill that mills no flour. They ship barley out now, but no milling goes on. The milling operation shut down ten years ago. It is a lonely walk from that lonely pier up to the Dirty Shame Saloon.

When someone opens the back door, the prow and wheelhouse of the *Joseph C. Wilson* look like they are right outside the bar. You may hear a stomping of feet, there stands a customer, an ore boat behind him, and you know you're in Superior, Wisconsin. It is a long trek up here for Konstanty Belich. He could freeze walking up from the *Wilson*. The snow is deep. Yet the graying, weathered shipkeeper, who's spent most of his adult life on the boats, will stand in that open door looking in.

"Shut the damn thing," someone will yell if the shipkeeper hesitates. Guys mostly stand in the doorway to peer in, see if there are women, and, if not, turn around and head to the Pour House, the Harbor Tavern, or the Marine Bar. I call the guys out looking for trim, "walk-throughs" or "lookers." As they're gawking or passing in one door of the bar and out the other, they forget it is January and February. You

feel the cold if you're playing eight ball at the back table. I, 3-D the bartender, feel the cold by the popcorn machine. I'm constantly freezing.

When he comes around, I don't know what Belich is looking for.
His whole life he has hesitated about things, it looks like. All week
aboard the *Wilson*, he tries to stay warm in the quiet, cold heart of her,
where he checks the valves and ballast tanks. Any water leak must be
reported, or serious damage could result. Suppose a heat lamp went
and a valve froze up and broke. I'm sure such a man, uncertain of himself, does not mind work where he knows what to watch for, where he
checks here and there, where he keeps a close eye on things until the
boat fits out again for the shipping season in March. Still, it is a lonely
job and a lonely walk up the plowed road that snakes through the fields
that rise above the waterfront.

What do shrinks call it—insecurity?—what this Belich has? I bet
that is why he stands at the door in the cold, not knowing whether to
come in. When he does, I watch him at the table under the mural of
snow-capped mountains. The snow on the mural looks a sick yellow
from thirty years of cigarette smoke, though Belich seems comfortable
under the mountains. They matter to a man ashore. So does the table
he sits at and the paper placemats with famous sites along Route 66 out
west and the jukebox and the click of the eight ball. On maybe twelve
Friday nights during a winter layup, these familiar sights and sounds
give the shipkeeper a place of his own on land.

So this is Konstanty Belich. His name announces that his ancestors are from some *place* in the world, maybe from central Europe, but
Konstanty Belich is from no place on land. For the past twenty years,
he's been a wheelsman on the *Edgar Lucas*, the *Warner*, the *Charles M.
Leighton*, now the *Wilson*, which he sails on ten months a year. His
home is this boat. Surrounded by ice in winter, but floating still, he
lives on water. He's done so for most of his life, first as a deckhand,
now a wheelsman. Even his mail is forwarded from the fleet office in
Cleveland. Who would write to a man whose one home in winter is the

Joseph C. Wilson and second home the Dirty Shame Saloon? Whether he's from Europe or America, when you say the name Konstanty Belich, you almost taste cabbage in your mouth—that and reasonably expensive vodka. Compare his name to my name, Dan D. Dunn, Superior, Wisconsin, born and raised. My name in the mouth has the flavor of dry bread. The *Wilson* is here for winter layup. Belich is laid up from his wheelsman's job for winter. I, 3-D, the man with the flavorless name, whose middle name is Doug, am laid up from just about everything. I am forty (probably fifteen years younger than Belich), my wife's name is Joy (Joy Dunn! I haven't loved her the way I should in years), and my latest woman, Bev, won't see me. When I was over there last night, the smell of aromatic pipe tobacco made me sad. I had to knock and knock before she let me in. By then the pipe smoker was gone.

You can't blame an older man alone on a huge ore carrier for wanting to come among people once a week. Some ore boats are 1,000-footers. You can't blame me for wanting to see Bev, my girlfriend, though she's told me, "This is the last time I let you in."

"Who's been smoking Carter Hall?" I asked.

"No one. I want you to go," she said, folding a grocery bag to put in the cabinet above the kitchen sink. The blue vein in her temple throbbed. "I let you in to get your stuff."

"I could clean off this table with one sweep of the hand. Your sugar bowl would break. The sugar would go everywhere," I told her.

"If you do, I'll call the police," she said.

As usual, I left her apartment and hoped for better treatment later. After half an hour, I called her on the phone. "Bev?" I said, pleading. "I'm sorry I acted up. I didn't mean anything. Can you pick up the telephone? I know you're there. There's no shame in being in love. Pick up the phone, though," I said.

At 806 feet, the *Wilson* carries thirty thousand tons, has a seventy-ive-foot beam, is thirty-eight feet deep. With the price of steel so low, it would be pointless for the company to load the *Wilson* at the Burlington Northern dock in Allouez for another trip. There is a week left in the shipping season, time enough for her to go down and back before the Soo Locks close. But at steel mills on the lower lakes, the taconite is stockpiled as high as mountains. You read about it in the Duluth paper. From here to Ashtabula, it's 878 miles, a long way to travel for something you already have stockpiled on the Lake Erie waterfront.

What do I, 3-D, have? I have Joy, though despite her name there's precious little of that left. Thanks to my aunt Ethel, I have a job tending bar. I still hope to get Bev back. She uses the Thigh Master I bought her. I had another girlfriend, Delores. She used the Bun and Thigh Master I got her one Christmas. Bev won't see me because she's wised up. Delores wouldn't see me because I never took her anywhere. Before that, it was Carole, Lulu, Monique.

Thankfully, I haven't got as many years on me as the shipkeeper. I try to be friendly to him, to all customers except the lookers and walk-throughs that smart off to me. What else do I have? I will say again: I have Joy Dunn, my wife. I try to love her. This isn't easy when I am interested in other women. One of my old girlfriends hangs out at the Dugout, one at the Capri Bar. I am known in these and other bars—3-D is known—so that no one yells "Close the door on your way out" when *I* walk through. Bev's told me that I have sultry good looks and boyish charm. If I shave at four, by midnight I'll have a hint of a shadow above my lips, around my chin. My eyebrows are black, my hair is shiny black beneath the lights of the back bar. My one worry besides Bev is a widow's peak. It starts to the right of the center of my forehead, a half-inch-square patch of white scalp. Because I comb my hair back, and it is full, thick, black, and rich, I cannot cover the space. I am forty. Is it my fault, Joy's, or both of ours that, widow's peak and all, I hang around the Capri, the Heartbreak Hotel, or the Dugout when I should be home?

Tonight, a working night for me, Belich has his beers, then orders a fish fry. Sophie is responsible for waiting on tables in the bar part of the Dirty Shame. When she's busy, I'll take an order.

"Lemon or tartar sauce with that?" I ask Belich. "How's things on the boat down there?"

"Shipshape."

"Baked potato?"

"Fries."

"Catholic Extension calendar with your meal?"

"Sure. Something to look at," he says.

Sophie grabs a bundle of them at New Year's Mass. She thinks she can do Christian witness in here. They are fun to look at when you're not busy. The theme of the last few calendars—that would be for 1988, '89, and '90—has been "Patron Saints for Our Times." One saint per month has a painting devoted to it. Among other special features, St. Patrick is the patron saint of excluded people, which is not 3-D; I'm not excluded. The apostle Matthew is the patron saint of money managers and stockbrokers; St. Anne is the patron saint of mothers, pregnancy, virility (virile, that's me; I have three sons); Clare of Assisi of good weather, telephones, laundry workers; St. Thérèse of Lisieux of AIDS sufferers (she's no patron of mine).

Seeing I am unkind sometimes to my wife for reasons that are private, a person will laugh at my religious aspirations and beliefs. But here is the belief: It was November seventeenth, two months ago, the day the calendar says honors St. Elizabeth of Hungary, when she actually walks in, Elizabeth of Hungary, at nine o'clock. How do I know it is her? She had maybe a Hungarian accent, she was with a quiet man who couldn't hear, and she carried an armful of roses. I have pieced this together about St. Elizabeth from Sophie's 1989 calendar where it says: *The saint is the patron of bakers, charitable workers, the homeless, hospitals, widows, nursing homes, exiles, the falsely accused.* For November of that year, there is a painting in the calendar, "Saint Elizabeth of Hungary Healing the Lepers."

The Tavern League of Douglas County allows rose girls to sell in the bars. Unlike this saint, usually a younger woman will walk into the smoke of the Dirty Shame Saloon and ask each customer, "Would you like to buy a rose?" You buy or she smiles at another customer and leaves you for Vic Rantala or Jim Malewski, the next guy on a barstool. In a minute, she's out the door seven or ten dollars richer. It is a cold business to tempt men. That's why they usually hire twenty-two- and twenty-three-year-olds to do it, this Elizabeth of Hungary being an exception. If you're alone at the bar, you and your bottle of Blatz, and a woman comes into your life, wouldn't you buy a red rose from her on a Saturday night? Would you buy one for your girlfriend if she was with you? I used to buy roses. Seeing the rose girls night after night annoys me now with Bev and me fighting.

But this was Elizabeth of Hungary, not just any rose girl who came in. In the calendar reproduction of a painting from the 1600s, she is washing the shaved head of a boy, maybe a teenager. Another teen is scratching his leprosy-infected head and chest while an older, bent-over fellow looks on as he walks past on crutches made of tree branches. Sitting at the feet of the saint, an old woman watches it all.

Later, when consulting the calendar, I recalled how a quiet man who came in with an older rose lady handed me a sheet of paper with an alphabet on it and different words and a sign for each. "I AM SELLING THIS DEAF EDUCATION SYSTEM CARD TO PAY MY WAY THROUGH COLLEGE," it said. "WILL YOU KINDLY BUY ONE? PAY ANY PRICE YOU WISH! THANK YOU."

College? He looked like he was seventy. Elizabeth, the rose lady, must've been pushing sixty. The word I remember today is "hurt/pain." That night I did what the figure on the Deaf Education System sheet did. I extended each index finger toward my heart. While she was saying to customers "Would you like to buy a rose?" I thought of Bev, my girlfriend, made the hurt sign over my heart, and the deaf man made it back to me as though he understood exactly. For the deaf, the "I LOVE

YOU" sign is to point your index and little fingers up and your thumb outward. When I made the sign to Edna Perzahalski, an old lady at the bar, she didn't understand. She gave me the finger. This was all before the *Wilson* put in and Belich came up here for his fish fries.

Do you know how a fact that can be important to you has been there all along, yet you didn't notice it? When you find out the fact, another plane or sphere opens up to you. Until Belich started buying roses, I didn't know, for example, that there was a story about St. Elizabeth of Hungary on the back of the Extension calendar I've had for a year.

Despite the opposition of her royal family and
courtiers, she tended to the sick in a hospital
she had built at the foot of the mountain upon
which her castle stood. Once when she was taking
bread to the poor and sick, her husband, Prince
Louis, stopped her and looked under her mantle to
see what she was carrying; the bread had been
miraculously changed to roses

I also didn't know that the woman who came to the bar selling roses wasn't Hungarian but Polish and the deaf and mute man was her brother. I didn't know Joy Dunn knew about Bev, my girlfriend, and had phoned Bev. I didn't know that Bev would pull so hard at one curl of her brown hair when she told me to leave the apartment. "That must be your wife calling again," Bev said. She called me "bastard married man." I have learned also that the sixty-year-old-but-still-beautiful rose lady lives four blocks from the Dirty Shame in the house of her mother, who has died. I have learned from Dirty Shame regulars that the rose lady is a displaced person from World War II who lived in Louisiana, where Polish refugees were sent in 1949 and '50. When her family moved here, she stayed there. She came north a month ago.

I am from another neighborhood in Superior three miles away down by the shipyards in the North End. I didn't know who the hell she was, never bothered to ask until the shipkeeper bought his first rose. I found out her name is Bożena Iwanowski. Once I started to observe loneliness turn into love, I also began to notice the job announcements on bulletin boards at the Soak 'n Suds, where I used to call Bev from, and at the East End Jubilee Food Market:

Check Out the Night Life and Get Paid!
$10–20 per hour
ROSES UNLIMITED

Next to a red rose with a green stem and green leaves, it reads: "*We are looking for ambitious, personable young women to join our sales team for rose sales throughout the Twin Ports area. Call Cheryl at 394-8076.*" To work for Roses Unlimited, I figured Bożena must have agreed to take the businesses that no young woman wanted by the gas plant, the ore dock, and the lime plant.

I do not know the love stories of others in the bar. To be as alone as the shipkeeper must be tough, though, I thought, till I thought of myself. I believe the fifty- and sixty-year-olds at the Dirty Shame—Ed Novack, Ray Reilly, Andy Swanowski, Belich himself—have given up on love. They are sailing far from distant shores when it comes to love. By the insecure look of him, the shipkeeper had quit loving long ago. Perhaps he'd tried too hard in Conneaut, Ohio; nothing had come of it. Perhaps he'd bought roses when the boat he was on unloaded taconite in Gary, Indiana, or Cleveland, and the recipient of the roses that time had misled him about true love. How often things like this happen to men.

Therefore, I was surprised in late January when I was perfecting the I LOVE YOU sign on old lady Perzahalski (again getting the finger for it), when Benny Adamczyk was matching his ma beer for beer, and when old man Hogland was playing a Dick Contino tune on the juke box, that the shipkeeper said to Bożena, the rose lady, "Will you please love me?"

Halfway across the bar, I read it on his lips, saw the word "please," saw the word "love." It wasn't ten o'clock yet when she'd swept in, looking stately in her long, blue coat as though searching for him. To protect him, I'd hurriedly flashed the "hurt/pain" sign I'd learned from the Deaf Education System that her brother had sold me for a dollar. By the looks of it, she must have been thinking a lot about this shipkeeper. I will always warn a man against love, for what has love gotten me but fifteen girlfriends and a wife I don't want to go home to? Joy is wonderful and kind. I am never excited to step through my own door, though. My joy with Joy has been gone for years.

When I told Sophie I'd bring Belich his beer, I heard the rose lady asking, "Why you don't want someone else?" Bożena carried her roses wrapped in clear plastic as though, before our eyes, she could turn them into whatever the Lord God wanted. As though Belich hadn't heard, she asked him again, "Why you don't want another woman?"

People might think Bożena was vulnerable. If she was, so was Belich. The best he could do to answer her, to give her hope, was to buy roses. He bought forty from her that night, fifty the next Friday, then disappeared into the bowels of the *Joseph C. Wilson* at the windswept pier, and she was lucky, I remember, to sell three roses in here on Tuesday, five on Wednesday. The guys thought, "Let someone with the money he's saved staying aboard the *Wilson* do the buying."

I imagine during the week before the replacement spells you on Friday again that you develop notions about love. As you do your inspections of the *Joseph C. Wilson*, you hear things in the chart room, hear them around the watertight bulkhead amidships or aft somewhere, maybe in the engine room. They are scary. The steel bends, the ice shifts, the wind whistles outside of the hull. I have watched ore boats all my life, seen them repaired at Frasier Shipyards, seen them lay up for winter.

With no one around, Belich must have thought about the rose lady when he inspected his valves and ballast tanks. The notion must have come to him that there was a chance for love. After an inspection below, what else would he do for excitement if he didn't think of her—watch TV, read a book, stare out at the snow on Hog Island, at the bay ice jumbled and broken now that the Coast Guard cutter had cleared a shipping lane for the start of the season? If he was fifty feet up in the wheelhouse during the blizzard of February ninth, he wouldn't have seen much more than we did on land. He must have concentrated on his roses, must have placed them in patterns around the wheelhouse or chart room. During that blizzard, I had tried to see Bev, but the snow was deep, everything white and fierce outside. Joy and I were trapped the way he was trapped with his roses, the way Bożena was trapped with her brother in the house of their parents, a house of memories for him. There is no escaping January, no hope in February, or when it snows on the fourth of March, Bev's birthday.

Later in the month, at least we are moving toward the shipping season. The waterfront wakes up. The *Wilson* and other vessels start fitting out. A warm day helps the ice melt on the bay. Lake Superior is blue beyond the Point. At the Dirty Shame, dripping icicles hang from the roof.

When I saw Bev at noon on March seventeenth, I'd forgotten my sunglasses. The bright sun on the snowbanks was blinding. "Will you love me? Please?" I asked her. "St. Patrick is the patron saint of excluded people."

"You sure appear out of nowhere," she said.

She was in a hurry, as though a lifetime had come between us. I was probably imagining it, but it looked like she was making the "Sorry" sign toward me as though she had no time for Dan D. Dunn. I couldn't keep up with her. That's how fast she walked. I told myself I've breathed so much smoke at work my lungs have gone bad. I can't run anymore. I'd drunk too much on nights off.

On the way back to my car, I stepped in a puddle. Water covered my shoes. I stomped them on the pavement. By the time I got to Tower Avenue, I'd lost track of her. I was panting when I got out of the car to look for her. No Bev.

At the pier, more trucks and cars lined up each day. Belich would miss this Friday at the Dirty Shame. Maybe he'd stayed away to protect himself from love. I checked the sign on the Deaf Education System sheet to see if I was right about what Bev had said to me: "Sorry" is a fist run in circles around the heart.

"Where is Mr. Belich?" Bożena, St. Elizabeth of Hungary, asked at nine o'clock on the night I realized I couldn't keep up with Bev. The place was crowded, noisy. Bożena's arms were full of roses five days before the *Wilson* sailed.

"Sorry," I told her. I gave her the sign Bev had given me. After loading taconite at the BN dock in the Allouez neighborhood, the *Wilson*, I heard, would leave for Nanticoke on Wednesday. On her black, steel hull, someone should paint one large "SORRY" sign surrounded by a hundred "HURT/PAIN" signs. That "HURT/PAIN/SORRY" vessel departing Superior should sail to every port on the lower lakes where a lover has been blue. The *Wilson* could lie at anchor off of the Lake Erie shore. Seeing her, everyone would take heed. The man in Tonawanda would think twice about falling in love. The woman in Sandusky would realize love is not for her. All of us, all lovers and potential lovers (in order to see the pain that comes from love) should see the boat as she sails away in the moonlight. It should be required before loving someone. In Port Huron, Grind Stone City, Alpena, up and down the Lake Huron shore, dreamers would awake. The dream over, the dreamer would realize the lover who was gone had left a month ago already. In Michigan City, Gary, and Chicago, people would know there was no hope for love. In the Port of Milwaukee, hearts would break if they didn't heed carefully the "HURT/PAIN/SORRY" sign.

When Bożena returned to the Dirty Shame at midnight, she had too many roses left. With the crowd pushing in, everybody yelling for drinks, I had no time to signal her. On the jukebox, someone played the Blasters' "One Red Rose."

"Where is the shipkeeper?" she asked.

"Who?" asked Sophie, yelling over the noise and music.

"She said 'Where's the shipkeeper Belich?'" I told her.

"Why didn't she say so?" Sophie said, growing crabby as the night wore on. With every order, she handed out an Extension calendar.

"I'm sorry," I told Bożena. "Sorry about love. At least it isn't cold out for you tonight."

She didn't signal me back over the noise. I've never seen a woman look around like she did. She was lost without Belich. She'd grown accustomed to seeing him beneath the smoke-stained mountains. I will admit Bożena is elegant. That is the draw of a rose seller, to hint to you that something more will happen if you buy the rose. Belich had believed something would happen and had retreated to the "HURT/ PAIN/SORRY" boat. This was his payoff for believing in love after years away from it: to stay aboard the *Wilson*. I am sure he was afraid of the Deaf Education System sign I'd tried perfecting on Mrs. Perzahalski, for there was no Belich this night, no Belich for a couple of nights. Had there ever been a shipkeeper Belich? I wondered. Nothing Saturday. Nothing Sunday. Walking in the front door to work on Monday, I headed straight through to peer out the back door to see if the *Wilson* was still here.

Much activity surrounds a vessel fitting out for the shipping season: her running lights are on a couple nights before she leaves; her engines are running; thick, black smoke is rising from her stack; supply trucks, electricians, men to check the freezers in the galley come and go. I might not see Belich again. It would serve Bożena right if he sailed back into his loneliness. He'd been telling Bożena he didn't know if he'd stay on the *Wilson* as wheelsman. He couldn't decide. But o course he would, I thought. A vessel can't wait until right before sailing to learn who her wheelsman is. He had to have made plans to stay on.

On the other hand, they were in love, so how could he sail away from her? He had everything I, 3-D, didn't. No matter how he'd tried to hide his happiness, he wasn't able to, not from me. Part of his happiness was caused by the return of spring. Part of it, most of it, I think, was caused by the thawing of his heart. For two months—who knows for how many years before then?—he'd kept up his guard. Now in March there was much being risked. A man truly in love would have to leave the *Wilson*.

I had my own heart to think about, broken as it was. "Can you pick up the phone, Bev? Just once answer a call," I was saying over the pay phone in the bar. As I listened and waited, Bożena Iwanowski came in with her roses.

"Help me," she said. She gave me a rose. On the jukebox, I played the Blasters' song where it says, "One red rose on a new black dress, crushing it between our chests." She didn't know what was going on with the shipkeeper. Everything was in motion on the pier, she said. The floodlights made it look like daytime surrounded by night down there. The tug *Louisiana* was waiting.

I'd missed Bev so much that afternoon and the nights before that I'd asked God to help me, but God was helping only Belich tonight. I didn't think I could live anymore. A mist was falling. Bożena wanted me to accompany her to the pier. She was dressed up to sell roses. She had been crying. There is no mistaking when a vessel is sailing. I'd thought the *Wilson* wasn't leaving for two days, but Bożena said she heard the crew talking on deck, heard the *Wilson*'s engines, heard chains pulling up the gangway, then stopping.

Until a few years ago, three oil storage tanks stood down there. They are gone now. The earth berm that had surrounded them has been bulldozed. With the March thaw, Bożena would get her shoes dirty on the service road the cars and trucks took to the pier. My shoes would get wet the way they had when I'd looked for Bev. Maybe Bożena could sell her roses.

When I turned around, she had slipped away into the dark outside of the Dirty Shame Saloon. Like my girlfriend, who couldn't wait for 3-D Dunn to decide whether to leave his wife, the rose lady had walked away on me, too. Dan D. Dunn never makes up his mind. I wanted to hear the Blasters. When I walked out of the bar, telling Sophie to cover for me by serving drinks to customers, it was dark except for the commotion down at the pier. "Bożena!" I called. Going to look for her, I came upon a rose every twenty feet. What good were roses to me? Far ahead, I thought I heard her saying, "Help me," though it could have meant something different in Polish. We could hear the gangway going up for good, hear the pulley chain's steady clank. The *Wilson*'s bow thrusters would ease her from the pier for the tug to do its work. What about Belich?

"Bożena!" I yelled again.

How could she see me? Trying to watch where I was going and to pick up her roses, I was panting, as though it was Bev I was following. Love never turns out right. Bożena must be running down there to try to keep the *Wilson* from sailing, I thought.

Then I saw him. At first I figured it was John Gordon wandering around here, but it was the shipkeeper walking out from the shadows through the March mist that would coat everything in ice if the temperature dropped a degree. What good could love do Belich at his age? I wondered. What good would it do him to witness the miracle of St. Elizabeth turning bread into roses? Who could feed such a sorry man? What love would satisfy him? I must have been thinking how I'd feel if I was Belich.

They hugged in a way I've never seen, Bożena and the shipkeeper. As though the mist and chill air, the night and their future, didn't worry them, they headed to the Dirty Shame Saloon. In this lost, hungry world, they had found each other, two people older than me. Having them around meant I would have to serve their drinks. If they ate, I'd bring bread. Sophie could do the rest of the serving. I'd be too heartbroken to wait on them. After saying, "I love you, Bev. It's hopeless for me," in the bathroom mirror, I'd be making the "SORRY" sign over my heart all night—or the "HURT/PAIN" sign that circles the heart rather than points to it. Worse would be knowing that when they'd finished the Wednesday Special, which tonight is roast beef au jus, Belich would probably go to her house four blocks away, fall asleep after loving her, then wake up in a room that smells like roses to love her again.

After driving past Bev's place later tonight, I will wake up tomorrow morning wondering how many more years I can stand to work at the Dirty Shame Saloon. How much longer will I put off joy? Tomorrow morning with the *Wilson*, the "HURT/PAIN/SORRY" boat, loaded with taconite, I'll do something loving. I'll present my wife the one red rose Bożena gave me. I'll offer it to her in shame and guilt for the times I've been unfaithful, the times I've turned away when she wanted me close to her. I will try again with her. I will try harder than ever. "Joy, it's yours. It's your rose," I'll say to her over and over, all the time thinking that if a man, starved for love, cannot have what he truly wants, then where is his happiness? I will say it to her anyway. "It's your rose, Joy. It's yours," and this time I will make her happy.

ANTONI KOSMATKA RESISTS THE GODDESS OF LOVE

The morning after he'd ogled the striptease dancer, Mr. Kosmatka received a copy of the city's Shaming Ordinance. Fearing something was amiss, he reached for his reading glasses. They were bent as though he'd banged into something. When he opened the envelope and found nothing but the ordinance, he figured that a city employee had neglected to enclose an explanation of what he, Mr. Kosmatka, was to be ashamed of. "Commercial and residential property within city limits shall be kept free of debris, maintained in decent repair—" On it went with no indication of what one could do to comply with the law.

Except for the Kosmatkas' garage, which had stood for seventy years and which they were soon tearing down, nothing on their two lots was in disrepair, and the garage wasn't that bad. Anthony Kosmatka had read that the city, having recently begun trying to shame people about their property, was going after absentee landlords first. The owner of one abandoned house had been ordered to replace and glaze broken windows, repair and reconnect downspouts and gutters, remove garage, and reboard the second floor so vagrants couldn't climb inside. "The code stays open until the violations are addressed. We'll shame them if that's what it takes," a city council member said in the *Superior*

Telegram newspaper about the case. Except for the garage that leaned to one side, there was nothing to be ashamed of at the Kosmatkas'.

The letter was addressed to Mr. Kosmatka at 2531 East Second Street, but with his first name spelled the Polish way, Antoni. He wondered whether his Polish Club brothers were playing a trick on him. Having for years served the Club in various ways, he was now its Sick Director. At monthly meetings in the Broadway Street clubrooms, he reported who was sick, hospitalized, recuperating at home. When he sent a get-well card and the seventy-dollar sick benefit to a member, this was noted in the minutes. When, as an officer of the Club, he visited lodge brothers in nursing homes or attended funerals to ensure that the Club's floral wreath and card of condolence had arrived, this, too, was recorded in the heavy ledger book. He did a fine job as Guardian of the Sick.

At the last meeting, he'd gotten a rise out of his lodge brothers when he began his report with a serious face: "Al Dzikonski got hurt."

"How?" they asked.

"He went for a drink of water at work, toilet seat fell on his head."

"Ha-ha!" they laughed.

Now he wondered whether it had been wrong to liven up a meeting. This was a problem at the Club. Though the guys were old, they didn't have to be humorless, he thought. In the dingy brick building two blocks from the railyards in the uptown neighborhood of Superior, Wisconsin, there they sat, chomping on cigars, complaining about everything. It was a club for old men. When the hard-of-hearing talked out loud during the reading of the minutes of the last meeting, the president had to warn them by banging his gavel. Their talking violated the by-law that states, "During the meeting, all members shall behave courteously." When guys came in late, they violated the by-law that states, "No one shall enter or leave the hall without the President's consent." Sometimes they broke wind without saying "Excuse me." There was no specific law against that, if it was accidental, but accident not, it struck Mr. Kosmatka as unacceptable to do this during a lodge meeting. A member should use the bathroom. The way the Club was run was a shame. The building was also a mess. Water leaked from the men's room sink. The floor upstairs was scuffed.

When Dave Pioro suggested the members meet once a month to see a football or basketball game or to go to supper, nobody said anything. All they wanted was to head to the downstairs bar—no Polish Club picnic in the summer anymore, no free turkeys to the membership at Thanksgiving, no Christmas parties, no dances, no Lenten fish fries. What was the point of having a fraternal lodge if everyone was too tired to do anything?

With increasing concern, Mr. Kosmatka, Guardian of the Sick, watched his lodge brothers growing old. After a man labors all his life as a car knocker at the railroad roundhouse, an ore puncher on the ore docks, or a longshoreman on the waterfront, he has seen enough of the world. Tired from his labors, it is sufficient for a retiree to follow whatever routine the day and evening present. Since 1928, it had been so at the Polish Club meetings—to follow routine—although Mr. Kosmatka would bet that members, officers especially, back in his father's and uncles' time had more energy. As they did for seventy years on the first Tuesday of the month in the Pułaski Room, the members recited the Opening Prayer, heard the Reading of the Minutes, the Report of Communications Received, the Treasurer's Report, the Introduction of Applicants for Membership. Since the spark igniting their last night out three years before, the Guardian of the Sick had seen a lack of interest in everything but the Green Bay Packers descend over his lodge brothers like the cold darkness of early November. No new members were interested in joining the lodge. Even the Polish seamen who, during the Solidarity strikes in the 1980s, had jumped ship to seek asylum in Superior had gradually lost interest in the Polish Club.

Late on the day after he'd gone to the strip club, a city truck parked in the alley. The driver walked past the kitchen where Dorothy Kosmatka was making supper. In the Kosmatkas' front yard between the house and the curb of the city's busiest street, he pounded a laminated sign into the ground with the address, phone number, and name, "Antoni Kosmatka," plus the date, "April 19, 1998," and the words "Notification of Ordinance Violation 15-770."

"What's going on?" asked Mr. Kosmatka.

"You'll have to call the City."

"I've done no wrong."

"So you say. You're not the City," the employee said. He slid the hammer back into the loop of his workbelt.

People speeding by were watching them.

"Come inside, Antek," called his wife. She'd pushed up the wooden slat that covered the three quarter-sized airholes in the bottom of the bedroom window. She was always talking to him through airholes—in the bedroom window, the bathroom window, through screens in the back and front doors. She was like a priest in a confessional, only better at giving orders than pardoning sin.

"It's somebody at the Polish Club doing this to me, Dorothy," he said. "Look how they spelled my name again."

"We can't have this," she said. "Too many cars and trucks travel past. The Polish way is to keep up property. A Polish person might not have much, but he keeps up what he has. People will think there's something wrong here—lice, termites, or something."

"Ten thousand cars a day go past," said Mr. Kosmatka, a figure he'd learned from another newspaper story.

When he called the city attorney's office, then the housing inspector's, neither secretary knew why he'd received the Shaming Ordinance.

"If you don't know, I'll take the sign down," he said.

"That violates the ordinance," both offices told him. "You better leave the sign till we check your case."

After another day of waiting, still no word came from the city attorney or the housing inspector.

"I can't stand shame," Dorothy said.

"If I do anything to the sign, I get in trouble."

"Shame, Antek, shame," she said.

"For what?

"For everything," she said.

"There's nothing I can do about it," he said.

"Shame, Antek, shame!"

Because of the sign at the Kosmatkas', neighbors called worrying about their property values declining. "I don't know what the sign means," he told them, beginning to think he was being shamed for something other than his property.

Not wanting to recall the fool he'd made of himself at the strip club by standing stupefied before the dancer as though he'd never seen a naked woman, he tried to make a list of less serious things to be embarrassed about. Sometimes he'd take the ice cream carton from the freezer and dig in with his spoon despite Dorothy's telling him to use a bowl and the metal ice cream scoop with antifreeze in the handle. Sometimes he didn't shave for three days, or he sat in the pew at Mass when he should be kneeling until Communion was over. Worse, when it was dark and no one saw him coming back from the grocery store, he'd pee beside his neighbor's raspberries. In addition to these failings, he thought of another, a group failing: it had happened on Joe Tomaszewski's birthday the second-to-last time the lodge brothers got together outside of the Club.

A Barbara Majewska and her husband had opened a restaurant. In five cars and a van, the membership had gone to Duluth to eat. Toward the end of the evening, *Pani* Majewska, the head cook, had come out of the restaurant kitchen, pushed her hair from her forehead, and said they should sing "*Sto lat!*" if it was someone's birthday. Every Pole knows the song: "Good health, good cheer. May you live to be a hundred years."

When she started it for them, "*Sto lat, Sto lat, Niechaj żyje, żyje nam . . . ,*" none of the members knew the words. Full of the Polish food and beer she'd served them at the Polish restaurant, and no one had been able to join Mrs. Majewska in "*Sto lat!*" "What kind of Polacks are you?" she laughed. Mr. Kosmatka remembered it . . . "What kind of Polacks?" The question had haunted him these three years. What had the Club become? He thought of Article II in the *Constitution and By-Laws*:

> *The purpose of the Kosciuszko Fraternal Aid Society (Polish Club) will be the gathering of members for mutual and moral support, also the fostering among us of the feeling of love and brotherhood, the defending of our American honor, and the celebrating of the principles and immortal deeds of one of Poland's greatest sons— Thaddeus Kosciuszko.*

Seventy years ago, in 1928, they'd had great leaders and done noble deeds; now they didn't even know "*Sto lat!*" With their Polish restaurant closed and the Majewskis returned to the old country, Mr. Kosmatka wondered whether *any* cultural activity could help the lodge recover its vitality. It was with great interest, therefore, that he read in the enter-tainment section of the newspaper about the appearance of a dancer at the Club Saratoga in Duluth. "Direct from Kraków. No Brag, Just Bar Facts. Miss Nude Poland." He expected the members to resist him if he suggested going to see her. A married man and Club officer, he himself should resist temptation, he thought, but if the members went for it wouldn't this invigorate them?

At the next meeting, he'd waited for the president to finish the first items in the Order of Business. When the Report of Special Committee came up, Mr. Kosmatka (as is required under "Duties of the Members") asked permission to address the brotherhood. "Remember when the Duquesne University Tamburitzans came by with the East Europe music and dance program, and we didn't go see them?" he said. "Rememb when the Accordion Hall of Fame had a look back at the life and work of Frankie Yankovic and Whoopee John Wilfahrt? Sure, one was Slovene, the other German, but we could have maybe learned something, and we didn't go see the display or anything. We have another chance."

Struck by his earnestness, the members put down their cigars.

"When speaking on a subject," Article IV reads, "a member shall do so shortly and to the point."

"No brag. Just bare facts," he said.

"What are you talking about?" the lodge members asked.

"Don't we give Polish sailors a drink when their boats are in and they drop by the Club? We have hospitality money. Miss Nude Poland, like everybody, needs hospitality shown her. 'The fostering among us of the feeling of love and brotherhood' is another reason to see her in Duluth."

"Is she here? Is she at the Polish Club?" asked lodge brother Bob Miernicki when he awoke from a snooze.

"We'll go to Duluth as if the Polish Hearth was reopening. She's probably lonely."

Five members argued that a Polish lodge should have nothing to do with a place that showcased such celebrities as Miss Nude Canada, Miss Nude Northwest, and Miss Nude Minnesota. "It's not fitting when the by-laws read, 'Members shall conduct themselves as gentlemen in public and private,'" they said.

With the Shaming Ordinance in front of the house on East Second Street, Mr. Kosmatka now wished he'd never seen the ad for the naked dancer. He should've expected nothing good would come of such a night for an old man. Leaving the Club two evenings after the ad appeared in the paper, the lodge brothers had stopped at the Dugout and the Capri so members could visit old-timers from the shipyard and coal dock before crossing the High Bridge to Duluth. At each stop, the Guardian of the Sick saw this fellow, a carpet layer who'd worked at his house a month before. Eric or Erickson was his name, perhaps Eric Erickson.

At the start of his last week of freedom, a bachelor party was honoring him by making the rounds of the old-timers' bars to laugh at patrons. Pointing to customers—hard workers from the cement plant and the railroad hunching over their beers—Eric Erickson's friends were telling him, "That's you in a few years." They'd no doubt stop at the Polish Club bar to laugh at customers there, too, thought Mr. Kosmatka.

Until Eric Erickson dragged the ball and chain toward him, Mr. Kosmatka wasn't sure why the kid was wearing it.

"See what they got me doing?" he said.

His friends had clamped a tow chain to his left ankle. A bowling ball rolled at the end of it. He was to pull or carry the ball and chain his fiancée would take possession of. They were preparing him for married life.

"How's the carpet installation I put in?" asked the kid.

"Carpet's fine. My wife had to have it. All I heard was 'New carpet, Antek, new carpet.' Is it heavy?" Mr. Kosmatka asked about the torture device.

"Fifteen pounds, not counting the chain."

"It gets heavier the longer you're married."

"I've heard."

"I've been married forty-two years."

"Why don't you try the ball and chain?"

When the kid handed it to him, Mr. Kosmatka found it heavier than he remembered. "No one deserves this," he said.

"I guess some do," the kid said.

The lodge members saw the party again at the Cedar Lounge. Commiserating with the Erickson boy, patrons bought him drinks. Given the kid's drunken condition, Mr. Kosmatka thought he'd seen the last of him, but by ten o'clock, the bachelor party had arrived at the same destination as the Polish Club. Not wanting to be spotted, Mr. Kosmatka hid his face and hurried to the bathroom when they guided a drunken Eric through the door and paid his cover charge. "I'll wait in a stall till the place closes if I have to," Mr. Kosmatka said to himself. In a minute, almost as if he were in another dimension of *The Twilight Zone*, he heard the bathroom door open, Eric Erickson scraping the ball and chain across the hard tile floor. From the other side of the partition, a voice said, "Are you in there? I thought it was you. I got used to your wife. It took time. I liked working at your place, though. Is that what I'm getting into by marrying Judy?"

"Sure is," Mr. Kosmatka answered. He tried muffling his voice so Eric might think he had the wrong man.

"Your name's Kosmatka or something."

"Don't tell my wife you saw me."

"Judy'd kill me, too," Eric Erickson said.

When the kid lost his balance and banged against the partition, Mr. Kosmatka thought Judy's fiancé would have hell to pay in the morning with that hangover. "Four days of freedom remain," he heard him muttering, the chain clanking. "Why you hiding?"

"I'm resting in here," Mr. Kosmatka said through the partition.

"Mr. Gorbachev, tear down that wall," the kid said, laughing.

When he stumbled again, the ball he'd yanked around all evening started rolling beneath the partition toward the Sick Director. In slow motion it came. How much the thing must weigh, Mr. Kosmatka thought at the moment of impact. A minute later, he stood in a puddle of water. Water streamed across the floor. Unaware of what a fifteen-pound bowling ball could do, had done, to a porcelain appliance, the kid left the bathroom with Mr. Kosmatka the sole witness to the destruction. It was like a meteor had struck. "God help me," he said. The wrecking ball had broken such a big chunk from the toilet that he was paralyzed by the sight of it.

From across the club, his lodge brothers signaled him when he hurried from the bathroom. Alex Wlodowski, Matt Guzlowski, Bill Lisak, Bob, Jimmy, and Charlie Miernicki—the entire bunch stared up into the stage lights. To keep dancers from falling off the stage's ten-foot-long runway, a metal lattice, rising two feet, surrounded it. Lifting the beer the bachelor party had sent him, pointing with the neck of the bottle to the sweatshirt he wore with the Polish Club's name on it, Mr. Kosmatka, shamed by being seen here, still shaking from what he'd witnessed in the men's room, called, "*Na Zdrowie*," a Polish toast, to Eric Erickson, who held the damp bowling ball on his lap.

Things went downhill after this. The Sick Director remembered a naked woman gathering up her costume, then disappearing behind the curtains, the music growing louder, and the P.A. system announcing the appearance of a great star doing more for diplomacy than the European Union and U.N. combined. The loud music swelled, a bartender headed into the bathroom with a mop, then the stage curtains parted, and out came the star from Kraków.

"Look at that," said Walter Gucinski, the oldest member to get around without a cane or walker. The Guardian of the Sick had never seen anything like her. Four red ribbons fell from her honey blonde hair. Her blue eyes widened and gleamed at the applause. She was wearing a peasant costume, a white blouse, a wide, red skirt. At the sight of her plump lips, Mr. Kosmatka remembered an old song, "*Dziewiczę z Buzią Jak Malina*, Lass with Lips like Red, Red Berries."

Except for the string contraption riding high on her hips, then falling in narrower strings to a piece of satin shaped like a heart, she was out of her costume two songs later. The string contraption looked like a slingshot. "I'd like to make a soup of that," Ed Miernicki said. Walt Gucinski sat dazed. His tongue lolling to one side, he asked her, "Do you have an extra set of drawers?"

Making his way toward them, the Guardian of the Sick heard his lodge brothers carrying on. The bachelor party was laughing and cheering, too. Suddenly, Eric Erickson, dragging the ball and chain on his way to the stage, grabbed Mr. Kosmatka's arm from behind. Seventy men watched them. Standing before what Antoni Kosmatka what everyone thought was the most beautiful woman in the world

here were the Guardian of the Sick in his red Polish Club sweatshirt
and the young friend soon to be enslaved in marriage.

Elevated a few feet above them, Miss Nude Poland danced over.
Before he could get away from her, she was squashing Mr. Kosmatka's
face between her perfumed breasts. His face sandwiched the way Eric's
had been sandwiched a moment before, she lovingly shook the life out
of, or back into, the Guardian of the Sick, who thought he was lost in
a steep valley of the Carpathians. When he began to faint from the
joy that kills, Eric Erickson, though himself slaphappy from what Miss
Nude Poland had done to him, caught him from falling.

After the caress of the goddess, Mr. Kosmatka's glasses lay crooked
on his face. When he stared through them at the Carpathians, he saw
beautiful mountains and plenty of stars. He'd suffered quite a beating.
What a fool he must have looked when he said, "Thank you. Oh, thank
you, Miss Nude Poland," and began singing "*Sto lat! Sto lat!* May you
live to be a hundred." He and Eric had been through it, all right.

In the morning when he put on his glasses, he couldn't see straight.
"I wonder if I need an eye exam," he said to Dorothy.

"It's time for that garage to go," she was saying.

She's starting in, and it's only nine o'clock, he thought. When he
smelled perfume on his handkerchief from the night before, he was lost
in dreams. With his hanky, Miss Nude Poland had been patting the
mountain pass between her breasts. He'd never loved the old country
so much.

"Don't worry," he said. "We'll get the garage down. The boards
might be worth saving. I have the phone number to see about the garage, but the number is fuzzy to me."

"No wonder. Look at your glasses."

"I must have sat on them at the special lodge meeting."

Before he called about having the garage razed, the mail came.
With the risk of car or truck accidents being great along East Second

Street, mail carriers drove down the alley to deliver letters to the backs of houses. His heart beat when he opened the envelope he got from the mailman. "Don't pester me about the garage again, Dorothy," he said, wondering for a second how the Shaming Ordinance he was reading could have anything to do with where he'd been last night.

When he went outside to think, he heard her saying, "It's not like you to talk that way." Above the airholes in the bathroom window, Mr. Kosmatka saw her wrinkled forehead, her eyeglasses that were fashionable twenty years before. He sure missed the old country this morning. Since learning what Eastern Europe had to offer lonely men, he wondered why he'd married Dorothy when he, a Guardian of the Sick, could have saved himself for Miss Nude Poland. Poor Eric Erickson, Mr. Kosmatka thought, I should telephone the carpet layer, tell him to remain single.

Though the traffic zipping by made it unpleasant to sit out front on the steps for very long, or to walk down the sidewalk, Mr. Kosmatka flew a Polish flag from his porch to honor his ancestors. As part of his Officer's Oath, he was sworn "to act justly for the good of all Slavic-descended people of America." And when the flag's red and white cloth grew dingy from exhaust and dust, he dutifully washed and ironed it.

On the street before the house, the heavy traffic dirtied everything—flags, windows, draperies. Highways 2 and 53 converged eighteen miles out of town, one coming west from the Upper Peninsula, the other north from Madison and Milwaukee. In town, the two highways, now called East Second Street, ran eight miles along the bayfront before crossing the Bong Bridge or the Duluth-Superior High Bridge into Minnesota, where travelers could proceed on their way almost with a sigh of relief, as the view along East Second Street in Superior was dreary: abandoned ore docks, flour mills, railyards, the oil dock, the lime plant. Near the Kosmatkas', several businesses made a go of it. Along a two-mile corridor were taverns, gas stations, a liquor store, video rental store, bait shops, motels, a discount bakery selling day-old bread.

When the sun shone and the breeze wasn't off of Lake Superior, Mr. Kosmatka would sit beneath his Polish flag. Still, there were the airholes through which Dorothy could reach him. "Psst, open these cherries for me," "Psst, go for the day-old bread," or today, "Antek, somebody from the City is coming. What does he want?"

When he'd received no satisfactory answers from the employee, he resumed his place on the porch, sat there for eight hours. He would stand sentry duty against the Shaming Ordinance, for himself, for the honor of Poland. Trucks, buses, every kind of vehicle roared past the flag, the sign, the forlorn Sick Director. What kind of Polack am I? he wondered when he finally went indoors.

"I don't want to listen to you tonight, Dorothy," he said.

He looked through an old Polish dictionary. "Striptease" was the same in both languages. "Stark naked" was *golusieńki.*

"Dorothy?" he asked at nine-thirty. "Would you dance for me?"

"What?"

"*Golusieńki,*" he said.

"Antek, do you feel okay?" she said.

Hour after hour through the night, he thought of Miss Nude Poland, of Eric Erickson and the ball and chain, of the word "naked." At three o'clock he reached for his handkerchief on the nightstand. The scent of perfume was gone.

Dorothy woke him at four. "Quiet, Antek, stop humming '*Sto lat!*'" she said.

"Shaming Ordinance," he muttered, half-asleep. "Love Ordinance."

At daybreak, Miss Nude Poland was on his mind worse than ever. After he'd shaved (and saying nothing to the dear wife who'd trapped him forty-two years ago), he took up his position beneath the Polish flag, a cup of Instant Sanka warming his hands.

Traffic increases at this time of morning. Everyone will see that my house is being shamed, he thought. I'll sit out here in case anyone has a question about it. During those two hours, Mr. Kosmatka also knew that as Guardian of the Sick he would become ill if he didn't call the Club Saratoga. Stiff from the chill morning air, he folded the lawn chair, stretched his back and legs. He *had* to talk to her. He couldn't live without her.

"When you woke from the dream last night, you were holding your handkerchief. Do you remember?" Dorothy was saying.

"That kid who put in our carpeting, I like him."

"What brings him up?"

"He shouldn't get married."

"You don't make sense."

"He reminds me of when I was his age. That's when I met you," he said. Before he went out again, he asked, "Where's my Polish diction-ary? I just had it. You're always putting things in the wrong place."

When she looked at him in the flimsy lawn chair they should have discarded, he was dozing in an awkward position, head nodding, chin falling to his chest, dictionary open on his lap. It felt as though he'd been dozing for centuries when he woke up. In Polish folklore when the brave King Bolesław died in battle, his spirit, together with the spirits of hundreds of his knights, were said to sleep in a cave in the Tatra Mountains. Having dreamt just now of King Bolesław, the Guardian of the Sick knew that if Poland needed him, he would awake and ride forth. Before he could call the Club Saratoga, however, his telephone rang.

"City attorney?" Antek asked.

"I am seeking Guardian-of-Poleesh-Club-man that was here," a woman said.

"Who's calling?" he asked, heart leaping. "No, you want the President or the Treasurer, Dave Pioro." Unable to think of what to say with Dorothy standing so close, he'd panicked and hung up the phone.

"Was that a woman? You sounded nervous."

"It's nothing. I might have to leave."

"It was a woman. Why did you hang up? We have a garage to tear down," Dorothy said. "What are you having women call you for? I watched you on the porch. I bet you were dreaming of her. You can't even stay awake. You're an old man, Antek. You get charley horses, lumbago. You take Beano before every meal, and now you're looking for women? Do something useful. Sweep the sidewalk. Go to the discount bakery for day-old bread."

"I've been to the mountain," Mr. Kosmatka told her.

When the phone rang again, a man spoke. "I was wondering—one of our dancers . . ."

"I'm on my way," said Mr. Kosmatka.

"Wait. I'm calling about a toilet. The dancer said you knew the guy with the ball and chain. She's right here to talk to," the man said. He was the bartender who'd shut off the water to the toilet and mopped the floor.

"Poleesh-Club-man?" the woman asked.

"Miss Nude Poland?" said Mr. Kosmatka.

"Who?" Dorothy asked.

"Beautiful lady, are you asking me to rescue you?" he said.

"Yes. Can you tell bartender who is, please, the ball-and-chain man?"

"I can't say who he is. I'll pay the bill for him. I've got to protect him. The kid's got troubles enough this week getting married. When I come to the Club Saratoga, I'll pay the damages."

"You're going nowhere. Clean out the garage," Dorothy was saying, face red as she tucked a gray curl behind her ear. "You're making me sick, Antek."

"She's leaving with her manager," the bartender was saying over the phone. In the background, Mr. Kosmatka could hear Miss Nude Poland.

"You mean I'm only coming to rescue a toilet?"

"Looks like it," the man said, calling to the dancer, "Where do you travel next, he wants to know?"

"*Czykago.*"

"Where? Translate."

"Chicago," the manager said for her.

"She wants to talk to you again."

"Poleesh-Club-man?" she was saying. "You are very brave paying for damages in bathroom."

"It's the Polish way," he answered, but the words came reluctantly, for his heart was sinking. "I want to see you, Miss Nude Poland. I can't tell you over the phone what I feel. It was love at first sight, wasn't it?"

"What does this mean—in the first sight of love? I do not speak that good English."

"I'm coming to you. I'm riding to you."

"He's going nowhere," Dorothy said, grabbing the phone. "How's he going to handle someone like you? He can't even get up from a lawn chair. Who is this? We've got to get our garage work done. We're shaming everyone."

"I'm leaving. I'm riding away," Mr. Kosmatka tried telling his beloved dancer, but Dorothy cradled the receiver to her breast. The Sick Director's face was reddening. His back and legs ached. He had a touch of sciatica. Pulling the phone from her, he said, "If I can't drive there, you have to come through Superior on East Second to get out of town. Look for my house. You'll see a Shaming sign and a Polish flag. Can you do this for a knight? I'll meet you out front. I'll get my suitcase."

"*Do widzenie,*" said Miss Nude Poland. She was speaking the language of the Old World, sounding heartbroken. She'd been in Kraków last week.

"Think of what we'll have together," he was telling her.

In the background, the bartender asked, "Is he sending the money?"

"I've written a check. I'll mail it today," he said.

Anticipating her visit, the Sick Director sat on his front porch when he returned from the post office. He stayed for three days hoping she'd drive past and have her manager honk the horn as a signal to see whether the coast was clear of Dorothy. If it was, then they'd stop to rescue him. To make himself noticeable he began, toward the end of day two, to wear a *rogatywka*, a four-cornered cap a person in the old country might wear. He'd found it at a rummage sale a month before. The garage came down during the days he wore the *rogatywka*, the city attorney called to say all was hunky-dory, and, short of dancing for him, the good woman Dorothy Kosmatka did everything she could to entice him into the house. But Mr. Kosmatka sat on, thinking of the morning he'd agreed to pay for the toilet bowl with seat as a tribute to Miss Nude Poland. As he dwelt on the beauty from Kraków, he'd not felt so young in years.

On day four of the exile, his mood changed. Age caught up to him. If she had driven past, she hadn't thought enough of him to honk, not even a honk and a wave out the window. Thinking how he meant so little to her, he told himself he'd been sorely tempted by a goddess of love, but had remained faithful to his wife because the Polish Club requires that members conduct themselves as gentlemen in public and private. A good-looking, successful retired man like me, he thought, I wasn't really serious about Miss Nude Poland. In fact, now I wish she *wouldn't* honk on her way to the Windy City. The Shaming sign can stay up forever. I'm a hundred dollars poorer for paying Eric's bill. I should be ashamed of wasting the money, but, really, a hundred bucks ain't so much to lose for a night of joy. I've saved the kid a lot of explaining and found a new friend. When the wedding's over, maybe I'll have him carpet the upstairs.

Mr. Kosmatka hadn't thought so seriously in a long time, but it kept his mind off of Dorothy.

By that afternoon, she had softened toward him. Seeing him out in he chair wrestling with his demons, she thought her husband looked silly in the four-cornered cap, the suitcase beside him. Still, he was her Antek. "Psst, why don't you drive up to the Polish Club? Stop on the way and get bread. What do you want for supper?" she asked through the front-door screen.

Without turning, he waved her off. When she told him she loved him, he waved her off. It had gone this way their entire married life: they'd argue, then she'd let him save face by pretending that he had won the argument when, to Dorothy, it didn't matter who'd won. He was a foolish Antek, everyone knew, even at the Polish Club, but when she asked him again to go to the discount bakery, she realized that she'd nearly lost the man she loved. And he knew he'd nearly abandoned his beautiful Dorothy Kosmatka for a Polish stripper. The look of pity he saw on Dorothy's face when she gazed out the window was enough to make him understand how God can punish such a foolish man as he was. The sign with his name spelled the Polish way was God's punishment, too. It wasn't a coincidence, that spelling. It was a holy sign. What kind of Polack am I, embarrassing myself out here, embarrassing myself at a nightclub in Duluth? he thought as he carried his suitcase with the Beano into the house where his beloved wife was cooking him a hearty supper of spare ribs, sauerkraut, and boiled potatoes.

And so it was that Antoni Kosmatka, a knight of King Bolesław if ever there was one, rescued his marriage by resisting a temptation most men would have succumbed to. In the old days of the Polish Club of Superior, Wisconsin, great men, noble men, giants in the earth like him, had also made great sacrifices.

THE WALLY NA ZDROWIE SHOW

I can't forget the sorrow of my lodge brothers when the doors closed to our beloved home. We had to pay a bill for a new roof, then the ice machine went on us. When the jukebox broke, we couldn't play "Poland Shall Not Perish While We Live to Love Her." Neighbors around 1901 Broadway won't hear the anthem again through the windows of the Tad. Kosciuszko Lodge and Polish Club, founded 1928.

> *March, march, Dąbrowski*
> *From Italia's fair shores,*
> *Back to join the nation,*
> *Back to Poland's broad plains.*

With all of us tired and sick, we couldn't drive or walk no more to meetings or to the Polish Club bar for a shot and a beer. I am one of the young members. Wojciechowski is fifty-four, seven years younger than me. Lisak is younger. For the rest of them in the Club, they complain, and rightfully. They say, "*Starość nieradość*, Old age is no good." They stay at home behind locked doors. No new members, no new dues to help us pay off the light and heat bills.

At the bitter end, Miernickis made up half of the Polish Club membership. If you had eighteen members present for a meeting, nine were from that family. Now with the Club out of business, they should organize a Miernicki Fraternal all to themselves. They could say, "If that's what you want, you non-Miernickis can have your own auxiliary." At every meeting almost, they won the twenty-four-dollar dues board, the eighteen-dollar attendance prize. Money goes to money. That one, Paul Miernicki, age seventy-seven, cried out, "*Jezu kochanej!*" when we closed the doors of the Club. We told him, "*Śmiech to zdrowie, a zdrowie to grunt* . . . Laughter is good health, and good health is all." Nothing comforted him.

I say, "Laughter is good health," when, in damp weather, my fingers are sore. My hands are swollen so bad it's hard to play the accordion. I practice for your mother, Tadeusz and Karen. In the kitchen, your ma and I sit at the table, look at your empty places, and feel lost. You are grown-ups living far away, but she puts out an empty bowl for your soup, whether *kapusniak*, beet, or mushroom soup. Someday, you will be with us when you have a vacation from work.

As I practice my old songs after supper, she does the dishes. Tonight, we had *bigos*, hunter's stew. It smells like meat and cabbage in here. Laughing, I tell her that with my schottisches, I am repaying her for the fine supper. (I tell you privately, it is not always much fun for me, Ed Cieslicki, stage name Wally Na Zdrowie. Yesterday I felt crippled enough in my arms and wrists that she had to get the accordion out of the case for me and help me with the straps. I played "Dreamer's Waltz.") I have good news to report, too, though—not just that everything is bad at the Kosciuszko Club and that my hands are sore.

Actually, I have three good-news things to tell you. The South Superior Market expanded the meat case. Your mother and I waited for this. Final remodeling is done. You should see in today's paper, it says the market has added "36 ft. to give us 66 ft. total, making us the largest full-service meat department in the Northland." That market is "Home to Award-Winning Sausage." On top of the counter are three Wisconsin

Association of Meat Producers plaques. In the "Smoked and/or Cured Small Diameter Sausage" class, the market won a Champion's Award for their apple bratwurst. I'll try to send the ad. We were first in line today. She wanted good meat, and, in the produce case, we spotted a head of cabbage. They have expanded the produce service as well. In *bigos*, you use beef, pork, white cabbage, salt, butter, onion, an apple or two. (Remember how your ma sometimes substituted sauerkraut?)

Other good news is that the church at Belknap Street and Hammond Avenue across from the courthouse reopened. Presbyterians held it for years until it shut down in '67 like the Polish Club has shut down today. "Enter These Courts with Praise" is carved in the stone over the front door. Who could pray in a locked building where everything sacred and holy has been moved out of? Now it is a Hall of Fame again. When you were born, it was a Hall of Fame, then it closed. Now it's open again. The words in stone have remained all these many years of the openings and closings. Today God's Courts are happily filled with concertinas, accordions, sheet music for both, a work area to teach how to repair accordions, and a place where famous musicians come to perform—Myron Floren next month. A woman named Helmi owns the Hall of Fame nowadays.

Here is other good news, my son and daughter. Your mother will be on local television on the Channel 8 cooking show out of Duluth. Next week's program, "H Is for Hot Dish," features Mrs. Agnes Cieslicki making Baked Noodle Ring. I like it served with hash. We'll get her a new dress and a trip to the beauty parlor. She's excited about starring on Channel 8, as you can imagine. I will drive her over, wait in the TV studio.

Now that I have told you the good, I must notify you of the hydraulics plant cutting back. Your cousin worked in its shop. It was tough for him. We held a benefit supper for Dave at the Club. Your ma and the ladies cooked in the kitchen there. Other women brought bread, cakes, dishes, celery. Dave's poor health was blamed on the plant. For twenty years, he breathed in the paint fumes. The doctor could do nothing. Your Aunt Cecilia is heartbroken, which is why I write to you in the Big Apple New York and to you, Karen, in Los Angeles, California, to tell you about Ceil Simzek. Here on this page are some teardrops your mother has cried for her sister.

More sad news. We have heard of a closing at work, but before I tell you about it, both of you remember: "Laughter is good health." That is what I do: laugh! I laugh as I sit at the table. I roar as I wait for a phone call, hand too sore to hold the pen I am writing you with. I remember that your mother and I bought you bongo drums when you were in tenth grade, Tadeusz. It makes us happy to think your sister already played the piano. We thought you needed musical training. The bongos lay on the kitchen table for your birthday. These would appeal to you, we thought, but you didn't like them. You thought you would play the easy way, just tap your index fingers on the drums. But the instruction pamphlet said the proper way to play the instrument was to use the side of the thumb and the little finger of one hand. You'd have to practice to get your wrists loose to play the correct way, so you quit.

Remember you were watching a rerun of *I've Got a Secret* when I practiced in the kitchen?

"Bring in your new drums," I said.

"I want to hear what the secret is," you said.

I ran my fingers down the keys. "Bring in the bongos."

"For what, Pa?"

You started to close the living room door on me in the kitchen. heard Garry Moore, the TV show star, say, "Enter and sign in, please."

"Don't shut that door."

"I can't hear the secrets then, Pa."

"No. At all costs, don't shut the door."

With me playing "Hoopi Shoopi," I know it was hard for you hear ing the TV. I didn't want you to turn it up. I was in my undershirt. was Wally Na Zdrowie back then. I sat at the table I write from no

Accordion to my chest, fingers running over the buttons and keys, I nodded when you came in from the living room to say the show was over. Your mother and you didn't hear a single secret. "What now?" you said.

"Play a polka with me."

"I don't know how. You just got me the drums."

"Play. Keep the beat up. Ready? One, two, three."

Tadeusz, beloved son, you looked uncomfortable sitting across the table, drums between your knees. You tapped away. I wanted you to stay with me on "Baby Doll Polka."

"Play one more song with me," I said.

"No more," you said. "I can't take it."

Over the years, I've tried explaining to you and your sister why I wanted the door left open while I played the accordion. You might have thought it was for air circulation between the rooms, but I didn't want us—not you, Karen, or your friends when they came over—separated by having the door closed on me like that. Those were songs I had played for my dear father. I tried to connect you and Karen to your mother, to your grandfather, to the old country and me, but you were teenagers. How could you connect to anything? "Come hear my songs," I said.

Karen and you would give no reason for your actions when you left with your friends while I remained at the table practicing the music I cannot allow myself to forget. This is what the accordion means to me, the Scandalli Imperio VII model I had shipped forty years ago by Greyhound from Chicago to Superior. I have gone to many nursing homes since then. I've entertained at Chaffey, St. Francis, Southdale, Beverly Manor. An hour of my music costs the rest homes nothing. Like in the old days, I am in great demand and have even received letters of appreciation from important social directors, and the people in their wheelchairs appreciate what I do. They request my famous composition "I'm from Planet Polka."

At the hardboard plant, we have made pressed wood for automobile dashboard trim and for other parts of an auto's interior. Ford has shipped our work to Mexico. This is what the accordion and a career of laboring at a hardboard plant have meant to me: I cannot go on without them. The owner of the Hall of Fame told me the white accordion keys are yellow from years of my playing. With acid she can get the keys clean of the discoloration caused by the fingertips. If I throw in the sheet music (most bought from Vitak-Elsnic Publishing Company, Chicago), she will give me three-hundred for the accordion. By the way, the Allouez ore dock in Superior could be hurt when Ford closes its St. Paul plant. At the dock, they ship taconite to steel mills on the lower lakes.

Beaten down by such news all the time, but smiling and laughing with your ma, I say, "Agnes, if she calls tonight from the Hall of Fame in the old Presbyterian, I will sell it to her. If no call, I hang on to the accordion forever. Job or no job, I don't want to let go of it."

Seven-thirty in the evening has passed. No call from the Hall of Fame. Helmi, the owner, is an ethnomusicologist. "What's an ethnomusicologist, Helmi?" I asked when I brought the accordion in to see what she would pay me for it. I still don't understand what is an ethnomusicologist. You and Karen, do you know? Am I an ethnomusicologist? Helmi has other Vitak-Elsnic sheet music. She has Johnny Picon and Frankie Yankovic records in the Hall of Fame.

Tonight's cooking show was "D Is for Dessert" not "C Is for Crockpot." I am wrong about the programs. I gave my heart to this accordion and, when I went by my real name, Al Cieslicki, I gave my heart to the job they've shipped out of Superior. Next week is your ma's starring role. "Agnes Cieslicki's Baked Noodle Ring."

"Next Thursday. Get ready, Agnes," I remind her. "'H Is for Hot Dish.'"

"I don't want you to sell the accordion," she says. "Why don't you think about it and have a bowl of stew before bed?"

"Are you crying?" I ask her. "I'm sure no one will call."

My fingers are sore by this hour of nine o'clock. They are sore as I run my fingertips through her beautiful hair to comfort her. I write this letter as Ma and I talk in the kitchen. She is drying her tears. Tonight's paper carries other news: "Superior's Koppers to close for good."

Koppers Inc. has announced it will permanently close a plant that treats railroad ties with creosote. The facility employed 23 people last winter. Although its ownership has changed over the years, the creosote plant had been in continuous operation since 1928.

(Tadeusz, that is the year the Polish Club began.) Hardboard plant closing. Creosote plant closing. Ore dock abandoned and closed. Everything closing, not much opening.

"There is time for *bigos*," your mother says. "It will be a celebration. No telephone call yet."

"Okay, I'll eat," I say. "Do you feel better about things?"

"For a minute, but there is so much to think about with the hard-board plant, the kids so far off there, and you maybe selling the accordion."

Son Tadeusz, when Helmi doesn't call me, I laugh out loud and startle your mother. At the stove, she warms my stew. She looks tired. She wears the housedress you sent for her birthday. No wonder she is worn out with the TV show coming up next week and everything else. Except for the arthritis, I myself feel pretty good. My accordion case is open on the couch in the living room. There lies the Scandalli Imperio VII. No one will phone me at this late hour.

Your mother's *Treasured Polish Recipes* says that in the old country, *bigos* is served at every hunting party. The book says a famous writer, Mickiewicz, wrote, "There has been a bear hunt. The bear is killed; a great fire is made. While the *bigos* is warming in a mighty pot, the hungry hunters drink crystal clear, gold-flecked *wódka* from Gdańsk." What they did once serves no purpose in Superior.

We have to count more on tourism for our economy, Tadeusz. We have in this city the Old Firehouse and Police Museum, the SS *Meteor* Maritime Museum, and the Accordion Hall of Fame, which the phone book says is called "A World of Accordions Museum." The museum "houses a unique collection of accordions, concertinas, button boxes, and other accordion-family instruments. There is also a library and a gift shop." Who is going to visit such tourist attractions? Downtown is a mess. You have to be careful the bricks don't fall on your head when you walk past the Palace Theater and Ansello's American Grill, but no one is calling about the Scandalli Imperio VII.

"This *bigos* is excellent," I tell your mother in order to pick up her spirits. Then I say, "Let the phone ring. After nine-thirty is too late for anyone to call here."

I do not know what is wrong with her. She can never let a telephone ring without answering it. Here is the worst news. I will say it again: I have lost my job at the hardboard plant.

I think I will play our Polish national anthem, "*Jeszcze Polska Nie Zginela . . .* Oh, Our Poland Shall Not Perish While We Live to Love Her." I will play for both of you so far away on one side of the country or another. I will play it right through the ringing of the telephone. I have said to your mother: "Open all of the doors inside this house, Agnes. Let no door separate us from our house and the house from its music. When you've done this, opened all the doors, then I will laugh and play '*Jeszcze Polska*' with all my strength."

She opens the storage room in the basement. She opens the doors to the bathroom, living room, and closets up here. She opens the bedroom doors upstairs where we have the second telephone. The phone is ringing. No doors are now closed. Nothing separates the old house from the anthem I play, "Oh, Our Poland Shall Not Perish . . ." "No, don't answer it," I tell her when she is washing the bowl I've used, and the phone rings once more.

"No," I would like to tell the companies that send their business elsewhere and hurt Superior. "No," I would like to say when companies close plants and put us out of work here. "No," I would like to say to the company that killed Dave Simzek. Instead, I laugh and sing. It's the Wally Na Zdrowie Show.

Marsz, marsz, Dąbrowski
Z ziema włoskiej do polskie. . .

I'll get a severance package from the hardboard plant. Eleven weeks of pay won't be enough. It will kill your mother and me. And you, Tadeusz, don't hold it against me. I'd never consider selling the accordion if we didn't have to worry about things now. I have played the anthem loud so that every room could hear. If we ever sell this house, the Polish anthem will remain in the rooms and closets of every floor.

"Are you crying?" your mother asks when, unable to let it ring, she picks up the telephone.

"Yes," I say. "I might never play the song again."

"But it is not Helmi, only your daughter calling from California," she says. "She is coming on vacation for a week and asks that I make her *bigos* and that you play 'Hoopi Shoopi' for her."

NORTH OF THE PORT

"**C**atherine," Grandfather would say almost every week during the shipping season, "come to the docks with me." Unfortunately, the oceangoing ships he wanted me to see would put in to port when I was in school, or they would put in late at night, or when Grandfather was connected to this machine that helps him breathe. Sometimes from the breakwater on the Point, we saw one of the ships, maybe the *Socrates* or the *Kapitan Joseph Adjuskas*, heading onto Lake Superior carrying beet pulp to Antwerp, spring wheat to Ghent, or scrap iron to South Korea. But these we saw from a distance. Bound for the lower lakes, they would reach the Atlantic in seven days, and Grandfather, who didn't care about boats that stayed on the Great Lakes, would wait for the next foreign arrival.

A lake boat's shipping season is longer than an ocean vessel's because the oceangoing ship must get through the St. Lawrence Seaway before the locks close for winter. Since they don't have to make it up the St. Lawrence River, lake boats like the *Edgar B. Speer* or the *Presque Isle* can sail a month later into the season than salties. Everyone in Marquette, Erie, Port Huron, Sault Sainte Marie, or here in Superior knows this.

By late January when no ships sail, towns lie idle, frozen. As though suspended in ice, lives like Grandfather's become meaningless. In March when the Coast Guard cutter clears a shipping lane, old sailors stir, cities, towns, and waterfronts stir—Lorrain, Ohio; Alpena, Michigan; Detroit; Chicago; Cleveland; Buffalo. In Superior, where our Chamber of Commerce slogan is "There's More to Our Shore!", residents guess when the first laker will pass through the harbor entry. The winner gets a free dinner at a restaurant and a night in a local motel. Driving around, Grandfather and I would observe the waterfront come to life in March as the lake boats fitted out. I'd make my guesses about the arrival of a boat.

Soon after the first laker pushes through the sea-lanes in the spring ice, the *Sea Spray* will come from Rotterdam or the *Helena Oldendorff* from Hamburg. Important officials like our mayor ride out in a pilot boat to welcome the captain of the foreign arrival. They present him a plaque, a key to the city, and a gift certificate from the Mariner Mall.

I always thought my grandfather, who knew everything about the sea, was like a port director or harbormaster when he sat at the kitchen table, the newspaper and his breathing machine set up before him. Sometimes I lifted the machine from the box for him. "Can't breathe today," he'd say. He'd wave his hand for me to help. I'd screw the plastic globe onto the motor, insert the two-foot-long tube into the side of the machine, and connect the mouthpiece.

I assumed his health problems were what made him crabby sometimes. He'd lived with us for two years since my grandmother died. Staying alone would have been difficult for him. With his breathing so bad and no one to help him do things, where would he find strength to go to the waterfront? His dreams would vanish without me to share them. Coming into our kitchen, he'd walk as though bracing against the roll of a ship at sea. His breathing machine reminded him of noisy engine rooms where he'd damaged his lungs cleaning motors with carbon tetrachloride. Now an ancient sailor, he hid in our house from the seas of disappointment. I hid, too. With Grandfather around, there was no reason for me to be lonely; but at sixteen, how do you convince yourself of this?

While the globe filled with the mist he inhaled, he'd say, "Catherine, get the newspaper," or "Catherine, get my watch." He often gave me a dime. He was first assistant engineer of our kitchen, and I loved him. He still could remember forty years before how triple expansion engines worked on Liberty ships and how crosshead-type engines ran on diesel-powered vessels. Knowing about marine engines, he could solve many nautical problems.

We'd study the Boatwatcher's Hotline together in the newspaper. For as long as the *Ziemia Białostocka*, *Ziemia Gnieznieńska*, *Zakopane*, *Ziemia Chelmińska*, or other Polish ships stayed in port, he was happy. He'd seen Polish refugees in foreign ports. In 1942 during the war, he'd written in the front of his Polish-English dictionary that his ship had brought cargo to Basra in Iraq, and there he'd seen a British ship with one-hundred émigrés on deck, mostly women, children, and a few old men—no young men, he wrote. They were dead or fighting in the war.

One evening he went ashore. From there the launch of the British ship took him to see the Poles who were going to board a train and be taken to Iran. Twenty-five thousand Polish refugees lived there in 1942. He'd heard that on the shores of the Persian Gulf and the Caspian Sea, the Polish Displaced Persons left their possessions when they went to be shaved, deloused, bathed, and given new clothes. On their return, their photographs, documents, everything, had been burned on the beach to protect against the spread of disease. The burning feathers of pillows flew along in the wind. This is where he stopped writing, and this is all he told me.

The next part is *my* story—of a Polish sailor who'd seen the burning feathers in Basra when he was a boy. The afternoon he came here, school had been dismissed early. On the Feast of St. Joseph, March 19, I remember Mother had told me to be very quiet when I walked into the house. She'd placed her fingers to her lips. Father was sleeping on the living room couch. When Grandfather and I had eaten, Dad, half-awake and weary from working at the flour mill last night, sat down with us. I remember we raked leaves after lunch.

"Listen," Father said.

Loose strips of birchbark tapped the bare March trees. I thought he must have heard a plane or a passing train. Shivering between the house and the garage, I heard the sound, but now coming from the direction of the bay. Swans migrate moonward. They stay there during the long, winter months of the Northern Hemisphere. Though it was early spring, I thought perhaps we'd spotted a swan, until I located a different bird nearly out of sight, beating its wings. I'd looked ahead of where I thought the bird was, but its falling was so sudden. The sound was in one place, then another. Father and I were confused by the sound.

"What is it?" I asked.

Later that afternoon, I talked to the nun at school about it.

"Describe it for me, Catherine," she said.

"It fell to earth like it was escaping heaven."

"The Lord's voice takes many forms. Let's look for a portrait. Here is what I think you saw." She pointed to a picture in the book on her desk. The description read:

> *Rising to a considerable height, the Common Snipe circles on*
> *rapidly vibrating wings in an ever-widening orbit. At short*
> *intervals it darts suddenly, obliquely downward, producing at*
> *the same time a peculiar, hollow, whirring note. Low-pitched,*
> *rather fugitive in character, the note is one of the eerie and weird*
> *sounds in nature, coming as it does from high in the heavens and*
> *seemingly from nowhere in particular.*

I thought it had been God whispering, I told my teacher. And then I walked the half mile back home.

When I got there, I was still puzzled by what I'd seen and heard. Grandfather said, "Do you know a boat is in?"

"Go ahead with Grandfather," Mother said. "You'll learn something."

"I'll hurry to get ready," I said. "I'll get a heavier coat. Wear yours, too, Grandfather."

From where we live, it is twenty minutes to the waterfront. Driving below the silos at the Harvest States Grain Elevator, we followed a road over the tracks to the end of the pier.

"*Dziaduś*" means "grandfather" in Polish. I said his beloved Polish name when I saw the size of the ship's black hull. I'd never been so close to an ocean vessel. Flying from its fantail was a red and white flag, beneath it in white the name *POMORZE ZACHODNIE* and her port of registry, Szczecin. Halfway along the length of the block-long ship, a gangway rose. A dirty safety net drooped beneath it. At the top of the gangway, five sailors milled around—above them the ship's wheelhouse, captain's and crews' quarters, galley, the giant smokestack. Grain silos rose above all of this.

Back and forth over the open holds, the grain trimmers on deck guided the huge chutes. Grandfather said it would probably take sixteen hours to load the holds with the hard amber durum wheat, eighteen thousand metric tons of it. The dust floating over the harbor slip, the grain flowing from the chutes, the hatch covers opening—everything was large, noisy, and dirty. Being there frightened me. The fine dust settled on our clothes. In places along the road we'd come down lay wet, rotting grain.

"Out on the lake, they'll hose down her decks," Grandfather said.

Dziaduś drove back through the dark canyon between the silos and the elevator in order to get another view of the ship. "I can't stop looking at her," he said. From a distance, with the Duluth hills in the background, the grain silos towering above her, the ocean vessel appeared smaller.

"Catherine, look!" he said.

From the bridge of the ship, a man shook his fist at someone on the deck below, the main deck. Though far away, we could see a miniature drama playing out. Other deckhands watched, the grain trimmers watched, as a youngish sailor walked down the gangway. "*Bóg z rodzi*, God be with you," you say to a traveler in Polish. At night I repeated this phrase, "God be with you."

The next morning, Sister unrolled a map in the classroom. "You are in eleventh grade," she said to me. "Tell the class how a person can learn about the world without ever leaving Superior." The girls who hung around Sully's Café in the East End laughed at the nun behind her back. My classmates never invited me places. They laughed at me, too. They said I was too tall. They said I was unattractive.

"We have newspapers, maps, and books, Sister. We have our parents. My grandfather, he tells me about sea journeys, like when we went to see a ship yesterday."

"He must know a lot. Can you show us something from his travels?"

"His room is full of souvenirs," I said.

On March 20, I brought a postcard from Tanga, Tanganyika; from Beira, Mozambique, I brought an ivory letter opener curved like a saber with a miniature elephant on the handle; from Basra, Iraq, a matchbox with an Arab word—under it, a lion roaring beneath a crescent moon; from Perth, a traveler's magazine whose cover reads, "A Series of Magnificent Views Illustrating WESTERN AUSTRALIA—with Scene from Its Cities, Forests, Rivers, Coasts, and Plains."

My classmates were impressed. They wondered whether the matches were good. They folded a sheet of paper, cut through it with the letter opener. Sister was happy to know about the world and said I'd taught her something.

Walking home from school, I was thinking about Grandfather when, two blocks away, I saw the sailor from the *Pomorze Zachodni*

I was sure it was him. Twenty minutes later, I was reading in the front room when I looked out and saw him again. He'd come up on our back porch and was standing at the door, the old jacket he wore barely reaching his waist. Shading his eyes, he looked through the porch window. When he put down his cardboard suitcase, a flock of gray birds flew away. *Dziaduś* shut off his breathing machine. Father came into the kitchen when he heard the knock.

"I was sent by priest. I am a sailor," the man was saying.

"What ship are you off of?" asked Dad, not thinking he'd heard right when he opened the door. Mother was preparing supper. "What priest told you about us?" Dad asked.

"I have been staying here last night. I am from Polish motor vessel. I will go to Immigration. Priest sent me to this house."

I didn't think Grandfather had breath to speak when he started in telling the sailor about refugees. He wanted to sail to Mozambique, to Tanganyika, he told him. Grandfather's old merchant marine uniforms hung in the closet. In the downstairs room we'd converted into a bedroom for him, Grandfather kept letters, papers, and postcards from Algiers, Genoa, Marseille.

The Polish sailor told us that after leaving ship he'd stayed at a hotel where a wooden sign read, "Rooms by Day, Week, Month." He said last night he'd felt a draft moving the yellowed shade, that the wallpaper was yellow, that the doors were yellow in the cheap hotel. It was so cold he wished he were back in the engine room of the ship. All night the seaman heard people in the hallway, where the faded carpet was yellow or gold. Some of his English came from the phrase book he paged through, *Samouczek Polsko-Angielski*. "Hau es yuur haylth in here?" he'd asked. At the door of another room he asked: "Hau es uur haylth?" He had knocked on the door of every fourth-floor room, hoping someone would answer. "It's bad for a man to be far from home in the world's most inland port. You cannot know how lonely is this," he'd said. He'd learned how to pronounce words from the book.

"Get away," someone had yelled at him.

"Stop the racket out there," another man had yelled from behind a yellow door.

The wind rattled the hotel. In his black sweater and oil-stained dungarees, he'd knocked on other doors. As he was telling us this, his face grew pale. "I am cold. I was in rain," he'd been explaining to the other roomers last night. "Will you pray that I rest?"

Somehow he'd made it through until daybreak. "This morning, hotel manager told me, 'You're illegal. You can't stay. The regulars complain. Get a room elsewhere.'

"'What does this mean 'regulars?'

"'The regular tenants.'

"'They yelled at me,' I told the manager.

"'You're illegal. I've read about you in the paper. You better get out of here.'

"'I'm Stanislaus Piotrowski, Room 412. Tonight and tomorrow night I will stay.' The hotel manager is angry but agreed to this. 'Just for one more night. You find someplace else tomorrow,' he said."

At the Immigration and Naturalization Service, Stanislaus asked whether everything in America was yellow or gold like the hotel. He told a translator he had a small book containing necessary phrases for his life here. They filled out papers. They made phone calls. Father Jadzewski, our priest, was involved. Father Jadzewski had told him our family would welcome him.

Wondering whether he'd disappeared into the sea or sky, Stanislaus asked us in the kitchen, "Du yu sy mi?"

At 4:30 when the priest came to take the seaman back to Immigration and Naturalization for more paperwork, my parents and grandfather talked about the Polish visitor.

"We don't know who he is," *Dziaduś* said.

"The priest sent him. That should suffice," Dad said.

"In Poland we say, 'A guest in the house is like God in the house,'" Mother reminded us. "We wouldn't turn away Jesus."

I went upstairs to look out the window. I thought he was handsome.

During the days he stayed with us, the sailor said the prayer before meals, prayed the rosary, attended Mass with me in the morning. I was pleased to hear Dad say he could live here awhile. To honor the occasion, Mother made a cake. Stanislaus Piotrowski kept the paper American flag she put on it. We spent the evening listening to the record player. Stanislaus showed us a stone he carried for luck.

Near eleven o'clock when Father went to the night shift at Fredericka Flour Mill, I heard a heat register open. If you knelt on the linoleum floor and put your ear to the heat vent, you could hear the voice coming up through the register in the room, whispering about the yellow walls of a hotel room. When I went down, Stanislaus was at the kitchen table.

I wanted to call to Grandfather, but he was sleeping.

"I am whispering to myself," the seaman said.

"Why don't you go upstairs to bed?" I asked.

"I am worried about America," he said. "I will whisper to you."

"No, I won't sleep if you do that."

He held out the lucky stone and said he'd brought it from a Polish village. He said the snow brushing the windows sounded to him like mounted horsemen advancing through history. Against the Turks, Polish hussars placed eagle feathers on their armor, on their tall spear hafts, on their horses' saddles. As the *husaria* charged through the century, the feathers hissed. The earth shook from the horses' hooves, and the feathers screamed in the wind. Telling Stanislaus I was tired after hearing all of this, I left him in the kitchen.

"A guest in the house is like God in the house," I said to myself climbing the stairs to my bedroom. Making an Act of Contrition, I decided to tell my parents tomorrow about the sailor's story. Drifting into sleep, I listened in the register for more of his whispers. I thought I heard winged hussars. A statue of the Virgin bowing in prayer stands in the middle of the dining room table downstairs. My parents and the Holy Mother would know more than a sixteen-year-old could know about what he'd said. My great-grandparents in the old country wore scapulars. They prayed to keep their souls from going astray. I prayed for him. I said a "Hail Mary." I said, "Don't whisper to Jesus what you have told me, Stanislaus." Then I prayed harder.

In early April Sister invited Stanislaus to St. Adalbert's. You could tell he wasn't American. The brown jacket the priest gave him was too small. The sleeves of his shirt pushed out too far. The pants were large. He wore no belt. But to me he was mysterious and handsome. I couldn't stop watching him.

"Ask Mr. Piotrowski questions, students," Sister said.

"Are your parents alive? How did you know where to go in Superior? Did you miss it when the ship left?"

"If I waited until *Pomorze Zachodnie* sailed, then I thought Immigration not so much problem for me. I stay in seaman's hotel before reporting to Immigration office. Now I am seventeen days in America. The workers of the shipyard, the transit workers, and miners have been organizing strike in Poland," he said. "To leave ship in America is strike against Communistic government of Poland."

"Will you write something on the blackboard?" asked one student. "How would you say 'He is telling about his journey?'"

"*Popwiadał nam o swoich podróżach,*" Stanislaus wrote with se blue chalk. He answered a hundred questions.

When school ended, Sister thanked him. A nun smiled, nodding t Stanislaus and me when we passed her on the way to the East End bus ness district, where there is a hotel, a grocery, the Warsaw Tavern, th shoemaker's, the ship chandlery, and several other stores and tavern Marsh marigolds grow in ditches and sheltered places. When it's st cold in the spring, the marsh marigolds are the first flowers to bloom. The chaliced flowers have golden yellow blossoms and dark green leaves. The southerly breeze that melts the snow and helps the marsh marigolds bloom carries the scent of aspen buds through the neighborhood. Stanislaus told me a Polish king let perfumed doves fly through his palace rooms. In the warm breeze, the aspen scent was delicate, and doves appeared in the branches of our fruit trees. Stanislaus came to America during the blooming of the marigolds when the air smells like perfume.

"I want to show you a hiding place," I said to him.

Where we were going, a creek flows through arch-shaped culverts of stone, then winds through fields before emptying a half mile away into Superior Bay. Thistles grew beside the path. The East End is full of fields, houses, patches of woods, railroad tracks. There is the hill above the bay. Two creeks wind through the neighborhood. Hidden by dogwood and locust below the embankment in one of these woods stand the remains of a house. Board by board, it has been dismantled. At the top of the cement foundation, you can see where the window wells stood.

Alone with me, Stanislaus brushed my hair back. I pulled thistles from his shirt. They were dry from winter. I was as lonely as he was, I told him.

When we left school, my classmates watched. We hadn't paid any attention. A neighbor lady watched, too. Confirming everything she'd suspected about us, she nodded her head. Thistles covered the sleeves of her coat. I had not said a word to anyone about Stanislaus, who'd been telling me for days that I had golden hair. I would let him run his hands through it and tell me this. I would hide in his arms and listen. The girls from school saw me hiding with him.

After supper Father told me to come join Stanislaus, Grandfather, and him as they played a game in the kitchen. They handed me a bone. I made them guess which hand it was in. The winner rolled it across the table to someone. As the game progressed, nobody talked. Grandfather's reddening face stood out against his white hair, and he bent forward with his coughing. Expecting whispers in the heat register, he'd look at the seaman, roll the stone. Except for a dog barking and that stone, everything was still by ten o'clock. "Problem with dog?" asked Stanislaus.

"It sees something out there," Grandfather said.

"It's Mrs. Dzikonski's dog," Mother said.

"Why is it barking? Trying to tell us something, I think," said Stanislaus.

"We saw Mrs. Dzikonski when we were walking home from St. Adalbert's," I told them. "Mrs. Dzikonski spies on people. Why would she do that?" I asked Mother.

"To see what they're doing."

"You're not like her," I told Mother before going upstairs to write in my notebook. On the vanity, I had a white lamp with a rose-colored shade. As I wrote, I didn't see Stanislaus in the hallway. He had come upstairs so quietly. When I saw him behind me in the mirror, I was surprised. He was always watching me. "Let me touch your face," he said. Mother was humming a song downstairs I could hear through the vent. I thought I should go kiss her hands and let her hold me to her heart. Stanislaus had kissed my hands once. Reflected in the mirror, with the dog barking outside, he was watching me tonight. "Let me touch your hair," he said again, and this time he whispered toward the mirror. He was almost as old as my parents, but the light from the rose shade reflecting off the mirror plus the shadows at the edge of the rose light made him look younger. He had blond hair. Tall, handsome, he wore a black sweater. I think he must have been a nobleman in Poland.

"We should run away," he said. "Tell no one I say this."

I laughed, pretending to kiss him in the mirror, to send the ki across my outstretched fingers. Safe in the house that stood in the East End, I didn't tell anyone when he kissed my hands or my hair.

What should it mean, a kiss made of air? If we were spotted in a room with a mirror, what should it mean to someone like Mrs. Dzikonski looking through the window at our reflections? The heat register in this room connected it to other rooms. When Stanislaus stood outside my room at two a.m., when he spoke from the kitchen into the heat register downstairs at three a.m., his kiss followed his whispers. He would whisper up through the heat vent so that it came through the register to my room: "'Fall will not grow what Spring has not sowed.'" In the daytime he'd tell me to say it. Sometimes he called me Katarzyna. I practiced it in Polish: *"Jesien nie zrodzi czego wiosna nie zasiała."* May was the time for sowing, he said.

Spring comes late to us because Lake Superior is so cold. Beyond the range of hills south of town, the temperature in places like Solon Springs and Amnicon Lake can be seventy-five degrees in the middle of May. Even inland two or three miles, but especially along the shore of Lake Superior where winter ice can be seen in June, no one plants their gardens. *"Jesien nie zrodzi czego wiosna nie zasiała."*

"Nothing grows now. This is not Poland," I told him.

Even in May you wonder when winter will go. In April the streets and gutters are filled with the sand the trucks use on the icy streets. April is our worst month. With the snow gone, newspapers and trash blow down the streets in the lake wind. The grass is brown. It breaks your heart when it snows now. Tulips are coming up near the foundation of the house in April. They don't deserve bad weather. You think nothing innocent or delicate deserves to be surprised by snow and the blowing wind.

"We should run away," Stanislaus would say when he came to meet me at school or when I got home. He would say it in secret.

I wasn't sorry I'd pretended to kiss him that night. Who else did I have when no one at school but the nun would talk to me? I wrote in my diary that Stanislaus loves me. My life is drawn toward him. I cannot stop what the Lord has set in motion. I can't stop the people coming to America, the steep fall of the bird from the blustery sky, the freezing and thawing of the bay, the whisper in the register, the sympathy of the nun, the boats and ships in the harbor, the rose light of evening, the snow of spring. It is inevitable. The weather must change someday, I wrote.

Sheltered from the north wind by our back porch steps, Mother's poppies pushed up through the dark earth. Peonies showed their purple buds. By the side of the house, dandelions grew in the yard. There was at least a hope of summer's coming. Still, the elm trees of Superior had no leaves on May 19. You must trust me when I tell you about the land and the weather of Superior. I wrote in my diary: "Thunderstorms came, and in the morning the southern wind brought summer and I knew I loved him."

We had sun for two straight weeks. In time, however, in this northern climate, everything—peonies, lilacs, apple trees—everything will start nodding and dreaming in the fog. Church bells will be softened by it. Fog muffles train whistles. The grass and trees are wet with summer fog. We live in the fourth-foggiest city in the United States. The fog comes in June near the Eve of St. John's. After it has been sunny and everything has bloomed and the world is green, then comes the thick fog that conceals the summer for a few days the way a sailor might conceal his intentions.

One day Stanislaus and I were walking where the creek runs beneath the Second Street viaduct. We could hear boats in Superior Bay and the noon refinery whistle. The ore carriers leaving or entering the harbor are silent in the fog. You hear the low thrum of propeller churning the water. You might hear a deckhand tightening hatch covers. You would think such vessels would be noisy, but they sail silently on their way. You smell the paint, the steam, even the ropes they tie up to the bollard posts with, but you don't hear much. Then they are gone onto the big lake, leaving a smoke trail on the horizon for you to see unless it is foggy.

On the East End waterfront, the Northern Pacific ore dock rises like a bridge to an old land. Concrete footings, massive pillars, and beams once supported railroad tracks that ran ninety feet above. The beams crisscross, growing narrower toward the top. Except for the gigantic pillars and beams, everything on the ore dock along the blue edge of Superior Bay has been salvaged. A fence and gate were supposed to keep trespassers out.

When Stanislaus said I was what he lived for, I grew frightened that Mother would know I was here. Mrs. Dzikonski would tell. NO TRESPASSING, a sign read.

"We will go to Chicago, have a nice house in that city," he said.

"I'm too young. Don't say those things."

I carried a wreath I'd made of field grass, wildflowers, and willow branches. Herring gulls cried in the sweet, wet fog when he pushed open the gate for me.

You'd think the railroad company wouldn't leave a gate open or a smashed wooden door on a shed dockworkers once used. In this neighborhood, people open windows to let out the souls of the newly deceased, they lay fish over their chests to ease their heart problems, old women, Mrs. Dzikonski, Mrs. Iwanowski, place tiny crucifixes beneath their tongues to keep their souls safe from the devil. Old times hover above the neighborhood like gray birds.

Motioning toward the shed with the broken door, Stanislaus said, "Come in with me."

"No," I told him. "No trespassing."

"How we'll get married? You are lonely, too."

"I'm not lonely," I said. "Can I put the wreath in the water?"

On St. John's Eve a maiden who makes a wreath, places lighted candles on it, and sets it adrift on a pond will see—in the direction the breeze takes the wreath—where her husband will come from. My wreath floated off.

In the middle of the bay, a lake boat sailed toward the entry. *Dziaduś* would know from the Boatwatcher's Hotline about its time of departure, cargo, destination. The words "CANADA STEAMSHIP LINES" stretched across the hull. I could make out a few of the letters. The seaman's fingertips were tracing the outline of my eyebrows. He touched my blouse. A kiss of fog ran over the water.

Feeling chilled when I stepped back from him, I watched Stanislaus go through an opening in the cement pillars, watched him heading up the ore-colored path. He'd made it to the end of the tunnel the walls of the ore dock form when I wrote "love" in the air with my finger then blew it away with my breath. When Stanislaus returned to kiss me, the wreath returned on the swells the boat made. I thanked God. Then we turned and made our way home, where Jesus brooded over the second storey of the house. I prayed to Jesus daily during the summer.

You come to Him by entering the hallway where a French door opens into the living room and where, at the other end of the hallway, stands the front door. You walk up the stairs. At the landing, you take more stairs to the right and you'll come to another hallway as if you've risen to accept Jesus the Savior into your life. The door to the boarder's room was on one side, mine on the other. The large portrait of Jesus guarded my door. Soft, dovelike breezes whispered through the screen as I sat on the bed retracing the history that brought my young heart back through the generations to love a seaman. Superior's clay soil is so compact that water can't drain off it and can barely filter through it, so it lies—held dreaming—in clay: Old water trapped in soil we walk on kneel over, pray above. My Jesus. I dwelled on Him in my room as I do now while below Mother reads the newspaper, maybe looking for the temperature yesterday in Warsaw.

In my room I believed the breeze to be a seaman's hands moving the drawn shades up so he could look at me. Stanislaus and Katarzyna. He'd sailed over the Atlantic to follow the dance where St. John's Eve led the Polish seaman and a young maiden hidden in a dream. Wondering what was going on with me, the girls from school called to taunt me. Though I wanted to leave with Stanislaus, I couldn't. Jesus brooded over this.

A single, curled wire bound the diary I wrote in. The wire curled many times through my thoughts. Five hundred years ago, three hundred years ago, forty-four years ago when Grandfather was in Basra— the minutes of years were like drops of water. Where was Jesus when the seaman asked to touch me, when he removed my blouse? Where was Jesus when Stanislaus found among the things in Grandfather's satchel a card from 1943 that read, "SHATT-AL-ARAB PORTS . . . Shore Pass for Ship's Company"; or found the sailing record of a merchant ship typed on yellowed paper indicating the *John Gallup* left Abadan, Iran, June 23, 1943, sailed twenty-six miles through a crowded Gulf to Basra, Iraq, where she stood at anchor before unloading her cargo of oleo, canned meats, flour, ammunition, steel billets, and tires, then departed for Tanga, Tanganyika, to load two thousand tons of sisal and to rendezvous with the convoy? Then to Beira, Mozambique, to load fifty-five hundred tons of copper and chrome ore and asbestos. Five hundred years ago, three hundred years ago, forty-four years ago—what had happened to Grandfather in Basra? Jesus, protect me.

"Mother," I said when I went downstairs on the Eve of St. John's, "where did our family come from? I mean do we know what they were like before they came here or what it was like early in the century?"

"Just try to lead a good life," she told me.

"In order to do that I need to know," I said.

"We're Polish. That's what I know for sure," she said.

Folded in Grandfather's closet lay a map of the world. I would study it when he took a nap. During his sea days, he had written in red pencil on the map the names of other ships he'd sailed on, their cargoes, destinations. For B&L Shipping Co., he'd sailed on the *A. M. Worthen* with gasoline for North Africa; for International Freighting, on the *Abel Parker Upshur* with general cargo for Liverpool; for the American South African Lines on the *Vernon L. Parrington* with general cargo for England plus ammunition for Marseille, followed by shuttle runs to the Mediterranean. Sailing on the *Joseph Lee* for Smith & Johnson, Agents, he'd gone to France with general cargo. On the *James T. Field* of the West India Steamship Co., he'd brought coal to Genoa.

In an envelope in the satchel that'd accompanied him in his travels, he kept milreis, dinars, escudos, francs. I knew from what he wrote in a log that he'd left ship five times in Basra, Iraq. He drew pay advances three times. He wrote how he had to pay for losing his shore pass. On the back of a pass he didn't lose, the Conditions of Issue for Shatt-Al-Arab Ports reads, "A charge of 250 *fils* will be imposed if lost."

Other things in the satchel: seaman's passes stamped "Port Security Officer, Genova" (Genoa) and "Port Security C.I.C. Naples and Marseille." Admit into this mystery a letter dated 1944 and addressed to "Federal Security Agency, Social Security Board, New York 4, New York." In the letter, Grandfather explained that he was employed by the West India Steamship Company, War Shipping Administration, from 3/3/43 until 11/12/43. In Iraq he'd lost his account-number card, but the information written in the letter was correct, he says. He includes his Social Security account number.

Also allow into this unraveling of a seaman's life a bunch of buttons kept together by a black thread run through the eyeholes (from his merchant marine uniforms), the box of purple matches with the lion roaring under the crescent moon, the postcards I'd brought to school as souvenirs. None of these things made sense until Stanislaus arrived.

It is 3,024 nautical miles from Basra to Tanga, Tanganyika (a nautical mile, *Dziaduś* taught me, is based on the length of a minute of arc of a great circle of the earth). It is 1,153 nautical miles from Tanga to Beira, Mozambique; 745 nautical miles from Beira to Durban, South Africa; 8,860 from Durban to New York City by way of Bahia, "the Black Rome of Brazil," and Trinidad, West Indies. The train from New York to Superior took two days. Basra. What did you do there, Grandfather?

Think, I told myself. *Don't tell Jesus what you've whispered to me, Stanislaus. Don't tell Him what we've done.*

In mid-July we received a notice from the Weed Commissioner: *Cut noxious weeds and tall grasses in your fields.* Many East Enders live by fields. For a place of its size, twenty-eight thousand population, Superior has more land within its boundaries than any U.S. city. All day, Stanislaus took care of the weeds and grasses in my family's fields. Sometimes he'd look up at my window. By late afternoon, I'd listen for him at the bottom of the stairs. When I expected him to appear behind me in the mirror in the shadowy room, Mother would call, "What are you doing? Don't stay up there long. Supper's ready."

Sailing away from Tangier in the '40s, did you think of Superior, Grandfather? I wondered in my room. How far was it from the purple Arabian hills to the gray March landscape where Stanislaus left the *Pomorze Zachodnie*? How far from there to St. John's Eve? Can years be calculated in sea dreams?

"Mother," I would say to her in the kitchen, "how do you know what our family is like?"

"Try to lead a good life," she'd say, but before she could finish her answer, the seaman would say, "You have beautiful daughter."

"Don't dream. Eat, fill yourselves," Father would tell us and pass the food around the table.

By late July the fields were cut. *Dziaduś* and my parents went to the Polish Club to celebrate.

My room was dark. Long ago, a coal stove must have warmed this room. In the wall, you can see a circular mark covered by wallpaper where a stove pipe left the room. Moonlight slanted through the shades when the moon moved out of the clouds.

I looked around when Stanislaus entered saying he'd gone through Grandfather's satchel again.

When the shades moved, I told him, "It must be the breeze."

"Is it doves' wings?"

This was a secret password he'd whisper. He'd unbutton my blouse, telling me about doves as he slipped it off my shoulders down along my arms. With my arms free, I'd hide in his arms. I'd open his shirt, whispering out my life in sighs. "Tell me of the palace with the perfumed doves," I would say to him. I don't know for how long I'd kiss his face and say this. I placed my face against his neck, his heart. Had I done this for fifty years?

I taught him a song about doves. For a century, went the song, people came from Poland, girls who loved sailors, handsome men bringing brides. Songs like mine cast charms over dreamers who fell in love in the land of fields. The word "Poland" means field or plain. There was a plain, and across it beyond a slight rise, something was out of reach. There across the sea four decades, no, forty-five years ago—something out of reach. I heard a stone and someone singing. Soon would come the scarlet time. We were trying to be quiet. He assured me that if I was strong, I could leave my parents. I could decide to go, he said, but only if I was strong. I was seventeen now. I would have to write to them that the heart has no choice.

"For a person to be sick for love is not good," he said. "We must go."

"When?"

Before he answered, I heard something downstairs, the door to a closet closing, Mother's voice in the kitchen. They were home. Hearing simple things like this, how could I leave here? I wondered as Stanislaus slipped out of my room and soundlessly entered his own.

I put my hands to my ears. Telling myself not to despair, I found a tiny crucifix that'd belonged to Grandmother. I placed the crucifix beneath my tongue. Jesus would protect me. For a moment, I blocked out thoughts of leaving, but the crucifix cut my tongue. Dear mother always devoted her days to me, protected me from harm. Both parents did. Although Father was tired most of the time, I knew from his glance and smile when he saw me what I meant to him. I put my hands to my ears to block out these sounds, but there were so many sounds, my world blurred. Émigrés have reasons to leave. Loneliness is why swans go.

For the next two months at school, classmates hurried by, locker doors slammed, bells rang. During third period, announcements about the care of the soul came over the P.A. I'd daydream of the crowded harbor at Basra. When the loudspeaker on the classroom wall switched on during the daydream, I knew a message was coming. Rustling her papers, the nun would ask, "How do you nurture the spirit?" When I'd stand up in class to whisper the answer, the earth seemed to move. I'd lose my balance. Like Stanislaus, I was one of the *Nowa Emigracja* leaving home. Then the earth moved again.

In my room at home, I heard Grandfather downstairs struggling for air. I muffled my own breathing. I couldn't make out what he was saying. Then I heard "Basra . . . Basra."

Let me say in this diary that our house has blue shingles, white trim on the windows, eaves, and downspouts, a green awning over a picture window. A little over from the window, concrete steps lead to a sidewalk. Ore dust discolors the corners of the windows. In front stands a cedar tree. Each autumn Father wraps burlap around it so the tree will keep its shape if we get a heavy snow. In back are lilac bushes and an apple tree. A few blocks beyond Second Street to the east rises the ore dock with its bollard posts. Looking north from there, you see the two-mile-long sandbar separating the bay from the lake that Stanislaus sailed in on and that, like my heart this November, was freezing, unnoticed except by a handsome, blond sailor and the girls at school.

Now as a pale sun shone over the shadow-filled days, I grew uncertain of the uses of prayer. I saw the earth below. In autumn, swans migrate moonward. I was far above the earth.

The night before we left, fog set in. In November, our land is silent, colorless except for scarlet bushes called red osier dogwood. It is the scarlet time. Coming out of the fog as if to warn us, flocks of gray birds hovered around the yard, then settled on the roof of my father's house. All night their wings beat restlessly as if telling us to mend our ways. But we didn't change. Stanislaus slept with me, and I was glad. At dawn in black ink the color of a few birds' wings, I recorded in my diary how Mother in the kitchen was saying, "Let *Dziaduś* be!"

When I came downstairs, I saw someone had brought in the satchel with the sea adventures and in placing it on the kitchen table had knocked over the salt Mother was pouring into the shaker. In Poland, salt symbolizes trust and friendship. Stanislaus was holding his stone from home. All night he'd been with me in my bed. No one had heard. Now things had changed.

Grandfather's hair was tousled. He couldn't catch his breath. He needed the solution from his machine. He must have thought the birds had flown into the house to frighten him, that if he didn't say something he'd never breathe again.

"I had a shore pass. I talked to a bosun's mate on a ship across the harbor," Grandfather started telling us. "I gave him the *Liverpool Echo* newspaper I got on the passage over. Something's sick in my heart, sick and caught inside of me—"

I didn't know whether to defend Grandfather or to kiss Mother's forehead to make her young again.

When she said, "I'm getting my husband," Grandfather said, "Wait. I have to say this."

Father heard the commotion. How sadly I took his hand.

"We want to go away," Stanislaus said.

The earth moved at a crazy angle.

"What?" exclaimed Father.

"I want to take your daughter away."

"From her home?"

"Yes," said Stanislaus. "When I was a child, my mother showed me the cards that fell from a man's pocket. 'What good is the Social Security card of an American?' I asked her. From thinking about this man, a Mr. Kalinowski, Superior, Wisconsin, I knew the harbor of America I would have to come to. I will go to sea and someday sail there, I told her. Over years have I put in on the Polish vessel to move to the different terminals of this port. I have been in your neighborhood to whisper, 'I have no father.'"

"Sure you do. Everyone has a father," my dad said.

"What about God? He is your Father," Mother said to the seaman.

"God's our Savior," Father said.

"But I have no father," Stanislaus was saying.

"I was drinking," Grandfather said, as if everything Stanislaus told us this morning needed explaining. "I lost my wallet. It was a half century ago. When I got home, I wrote to the Social Security about what happened."

Inside the jar on the machine the solution bubbled. Through the tube, Grandfather drew his mist. The bubbling in the jar stopped, began, stopped. He breathed it in as though it would let him tell his secret.

"What's the problem that we can't get along?" Mother asked, as if hearing the commotion for the first time. She was angry for letting the sailor stay here. He'd betrayed us. If a guest in the house is like God in the house, Stanislaus had betrayed Jesus, too. She was angry at me as much as anyone.

"I came off of the Liberty ship *John Gallup*," Grandfather was saying. "Near the fantail hung a canvas tarp. There she was. Your mother has no one on earth. I tell her I'll take her to America off of that stinking British ship. I was married the year before. Your father was on the way, Catherine," he said, nodding to me. "Look at the memories I carry with me."

When the blue mist in Grandfather's machine was used up, there would be no air for him. He was sick, old. Life had been peaceful. What had happened? I was their daughter. I had caused them such pain.

"Here," Stanislaus said, producing from his shirt the cards Grandfather had lost. "Here," he said, from his pants pocket taking a worn dollar bill. Four decades earlier, the dollar of overtime pay had traveled through Iran with the seaman's mother, then by boat across the Black Sea, then through a part of the Soviet Union into Poland. The Poles stayed in Tehran, left, went elsewhere, made the journey home. The American dollar was now returned to my grandfather, the man who'd worked the boilers of the *John Gallup*. "Here," said Stanislaus. He gave us a letter his mother had sent in 1955 when *Dziaduś* could breathe. Celebrating what was called a "Five-Year Plan" in Poland under the Communists, the postage stamp showed two young men, one with a helmet and rifle, the other carrying a riveter's gun. "*NAPROD, DO WALKI* . . . ON, TO THE STRUGGLE," the stamp read.

"I found it in the satchel your Catherine lets me look into," the seaman said. "The letter says how is life hard in Poland. How my mother has hardly the money to send the letter. How after the war she returned there. A hard journey for a woman. In 1955 I am eleven. By this age, I love the sea. 'Can you send money? It is hard in Poland,' my mother writes to a married man in America."

"Grażyna, Grażyna. The heat was terrible," Grandfather said. "Grace was her name. We had four feet of privacy, Grażyna and me. I told her I'd take her from her ship over to mine. I'd do what I could to help her. I'd give her all my overtime pay. I'd bribe the cockney. My wedding anniversary came. I had a wife in America. I was tired of overtime Grażyna loved me."

Every line on Grandfather's face was twisted so you couldn't follow the lines to anywhere. Mother was praying. "*Jezu, Maryo, Józefie,*" she was saying.

"Something happened," he said. "She hung on me. I was rubbing on the contents of my Sanitube. It was a first-aid cream you rubbed on all your parts after doing something like that with a woman. I was thinking of home. I was fed up with myself. She said, 'America is Land of Free.' Sam, the bosun's mate, chuckled. I got angry. I'd never given her my name. She found it on a port pass or on the Social Security card or on the cards I lost from the wallet. She hung onto my neck when I threw the Sanitube to Sammy. After our love, I was rubbing the Sanitube cream on me.

"'Push 'er off you if she's annoying you and you're tired, lad,' he said.

"'Take her away, Sammy. You're the bosun's mate. She loves me.'

"'No, push 'er. Be self-reliant.'

"My hands were greasy. I didn't want my khakis greasy.

"'Go on! Push 'er. Push 'er, Yank!'

"She had no strength to resist when I did as Sam ordered.

"''at's it,' he said, quiet like he'd been directing me on a stage. After the twenty-five minutes when Grażyna and I made love under the tarp hanging over us, I leaned against the bulkhead. Sam gave me a rag. I gave her my pay. On the *John Gallup*, I earned overtime by replacing a blown gasket in the steam line to the main feed pumps. It was crazy. It was in the line of duty in a place that was hot as hell. We were behind these cans on the fantail. We were lonely. We fell in love.

"I worked with boilers. I'd reached a 'blow down' point. The blow down is the difference between the blow off and the receding point of boiler valves. Adjust the ring and you regulate the amount of the blow down. Too much, the valve simmers . . . too little the blow down, the valve chatters. It's burning hot in Basra. That cockney! All evening the night before I'd worked on the steamline gasket that blew like Sam and me blew. When I'm done working the gasket, I realized my cards are stolen. I'm tired from overtime work. I toss and turn in the heat. She

begged, 'Take me with you.' She couldn't do nothing to me if I didn't,"
said *Dziaduś*, sounding as though he was strangling on what he'd
confessed.

"Oh, God!" Mother cried. She called Father Jadzewski's number.
"Please hang up and try your call again," the voice directed. Even across
the room, I could hear a sound in the receiver until my dad took away
the phone, hung it up. Now the sound was at the window. It was in the
chimney, steady enough that you knew the sharp beaks would get you.
Stanislaus was pushing Father out of his way. I was running beside
him. "I have no father," Stanislaus said.

The gray birds kept Mother inside.

"I can't go back in to you," I told her.

When Stanislaus started the car, I thought how we Polish have come
to America in great immigrant waves, bringing the future out of the
past, great flocks of immigrants.

We made the turn off the bridge that joins Wisconsin and Minnesota.
The interstate highway passes a block below the downtown business
district of Duluth. Making late-season runs, lake boats wait in the harbor for a berth at the grain terminals.

I sat close to Stanislaus. "Do you love me?" I asked. Looking out on
the lake, my view drifted into the haze.

"You are mine," he said.

Outside Duluth where the interstate ends, the highway became two
lanes on the scenic route. He wanted to get away, to find a quiet motel
where no one would interrupt us.

"We will hide. We will go to Basra," he said.

Through a long stretch of road, the pine forests lay heavy with snow.
Snow often comes earlier to the north shore of Lake Superior than it
does to Duluth or Superior. Though the country looked wild and forlorn, it looked nothing like the shore of the heart that has fallen away
from love. In Lake Superior, the deepest, coldest of the Great Lakes,
the drowned don't rise because of the temperature of the water. It was

as if *Dziaduś* had drowned in the cold where secrets dwell. For years, Stanislaus had lived with the secret, too, until time for him to leave the *Pomorze Zachodnie*.

We turned off the scenic route. In the gray afternoon at the end of a road, we'd seen a neon sign. Behind the tourist cabins where we were heading, the waves broke in from the lake, then back down a sloping beach.

"Ten dollars a night," said a man at the desk. "I'm your desk clerk/watchman. See everything's right for you."

In cabin 1-A, the bedsheets were a dingy yellow. Only a desperate traveler would stay here.

When Stanislaus adjusted the heater in the cabin, everything would be better, I thought. Stanislaus would be happy when the heater warmed the room and when the heater's clanging stopped. But Eric, the day and night watchman, regulated heat here, so the metal banged again when the heater shut off to cool down. For a few moments, we'd have a rest from the noise in the tourist cabin, then the banging began again as the blue flame heated the coils of a gas stove that warmed the room.

We lay in the hot darkness the watchman wasn't regulating. He was Sammy, the bosun's mate.

"I don't like the noise," I said. "Can we whisper and dream?"

"Shh—softly," Stanislaus whispered, so I'm not sure I heard what he said. There must have been something about love in it or in the gentle way he touched my face.

During the night, I whispered to him, too, whispered his name. On the November coast with waves coming to shore so near our bed and with the heater waking me, I heard a dreamer say *Dziaduś* threw away the dirty rag the cockney'd given him in '43.

I couldn't sleep after that. I watched Stanislaus mutter and toss. He didn't say things I understood. I was thinking and thinking how we cannot comprehend a whisper when we're dreaming and it comes up a

furnace register late at night. If we aren't prepared, we cannot comprehend a whisper telling us what was buried generations before. How slight
the sound the secrets of the past make. Sometimes no one hears them.
But there are such whispers circulating in a house. Grandfather himself
was a whisperer, who'd been caught by a dream. Whisper to me from
years ago, Stanislaus, I thought. Whisper you love me. Whisper "The
storm comes from the sea, *Wyszła burza od morza*." Whisper, Mother
and Father, that Poland is an old country. Whisper, Grandfather, that
Iraq and Iran are old. Whisper that I have no one but the seaman.

In the tourist cabin we sat into the afternoon the next day. Stanislaus
leaned his back and neck against the headboard. I sat in the nicked-up
wooden chair. We talked about life, about winter. He was sketching a
picture and writing words in the phone book he found in the drawer
of the rickety bedside table. "HOW MANY WAYS CAN THE BOX
OPEN?" he wrote below the picture he drew. The more you looked, the
more ways you saw.

Eric, the watchman, wanted to know, Were we okay?

"We're fine," Stanislaus said, covering himself with the yellowed
sheet and rough wool blanket.

At four o'clock, I looked through the window at the lake. The snow
took time coming down. Stanislaus asked me to say the word "love," to
kiss him as I did. What gold was buried in America? Stanislaus wanted
to know.

No matter what we said to each other, I guess the watchman didn't
believe we were okay. He made the heater bang. Things were unregu-
lated. It was like a sharp clang, a BO-IIING sound. You wouldn't mind
if it were steady, but this impulsive noise—we knew when the gas jets
in the coil ignited that the noise was coming, but we never knew how
loud, how fast.

In the interval between the stove noise, the phone rang. "Who is
calling?" I asked Stanislaus. "Is it my father?"

"Here's one way the box opens," he replied. "You can believe I was maybe a nine-year-old boy sitting beside my mother who drove a tractor on a collectivized farm in Bydgoszcz. Otherwise, you don't know who Stanislaus is. You have not an idea where I lived or what is my authentic name."

When the phone rang again, startling me, he said, "You can believe I came to Poland when I was three. You can believe my stepfather was driver for the transit system. You can believe I lived in Łódź and in parades carried a banner that read, "TOWARDS PROSPERITY, TOWARDS SOCIALISM . . . *DO DOBROBYTU, DO SOCJALIZMU*." You can open the box. You can believe I lived here and loved you."

This time when the phone rang, he told me not to answer it if he was out. "You can believe what you want by yourself. Just always remember my love for my young Catherine."

"Everything okay?" asked the watchman when Stanislaus picked up the phone. "Will you be comfortable with more heat? I thought about checking on you. Your ancestors get in okay?"

"We're all in okay," Stanislaus said.

It was seven. Dark. The light in the world fell on a sketch in a phone book. The last light in the world fell on an optical illusion Stanislaus sketched. For me, the only sound left on earth grew into whispers asking, HOW MANY WAYS CAN THE BOX OPEN?"

This is what he'd drawn. In the box lay the shores of regret. There could be any number of ways to open the box. Look at them:

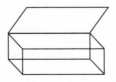

When he left the room that evening, I wondered how I could keep up with an illusion who'd come to me on the Feast of St. Joseph in March.

"Wait!" I said to him as he opened the door to leave me. "We love each other." The wind blew my voice back.

On the lake, an ore carrier made for port. Far away, the lights of Duluth-Superior lay surrounded by night. Trying to follow Stanislaus, I made my way along the loud waves. "We love each other." With no one but the dead to answer me on the windy shore, the waves pounding in, I called it over and over. "Wait for me!"

For ten thousand years, there was nothing along this shore. Not on this night. In the soul's voice, I heard Grażyna pleading, "Take me to America." I heard *Dziaduś* lie to her, heard Grażyna in Łódź telling her boy that he was born in Iran. I heard Stanislaus whispering, heard the whisper of memory. ON, TO THE STRUGGLE . . . *NAPRZÓD, DO WALKI.*

In the inky blackness, a north wind blew swells against a rocky coast. My coat flapped about me in the bitter wind. I loved Stanislaus. The wind said I did. "Please, let's go back," I called once again into the darkness. I made my way back to the tourist cabin and found my sailor in the parking lot.

In the dim light coming from the tourist cabin, Stanislaus said it was forty-four years ago. We could hear the night watchman on the phone in our room saying, "It's a mess. The whole thing's a big mess." He was trying to take the phone book for proof or something, but Stanislaus wanted it back from him. "It is the long ago time. I am a whisper. I will return to my ship. I need to talk to Sammy," he said. "I will have to regulate the 'blow down' point on the boiler."

"I'll get a map for us," I said, but Stanislaus slipped off like Grandfather had left Grażyna fifteen thousand nautical miles east of here. When he closed the door on the wind, the world stopped. I was alone in the room with the night watchman who failed to regulate things. I ran out into the cold. How could I sort out the seaman's whispers from the wind, the waves?

"I don't know where he is," I told Eric when I returned, frantic. "Help me," I said.

"I see what you mean," he said. He'd turned up the knob to the eigh and nine range of heat. I was pushing and fighting the motel watchman off when the car pulled up. The deputy, my mother and father, a priest. They came to save me from the seaman who'd gone back into history. But I wasn't saved. I never could be.

Mother was sick over this. Someone had spotted us and called the sheriff about a man and a girl in the tourist cabins. (I thought Eric had called.) Now Mother cried and raised her hands prayerfully to heaven. I cried, too, when the rescuers came. I didn't cry for *Dziaduś,* who was in the hospital, nor for my parents. I cried for whispers, for faces in mirrors, for the soul in its golden coil.

Day after day, my parents said, "Eat, Catherine. It's good for the soul to be fed." My father appeared as though he'd given up on life. He'd reach for a coffee cup or for the plate Mother handed him at supper, and his hands trembled. He'd shake his head sadly when he thought I wasn't looking. The wrinkles on his face, on Mother's, grew into maps each of them knew. "Can we hope you'll say penance?" they asked.

"Yes," I said.

I couldn't pray or sleep. I'd think of him. No word from him. No one to trace a missing person, a whisper. I kept thinking, night after night, that he was waiting for me on the docks. Like swans, we'd migrate moonward over the long, blue edge of the lake. When I thought of him, I listened for doves in the winter fruit trees.

On a trip from home some years later, I took an El train to Logan Square. Five blocks up North Milwaukee Avenue from the CTA stop, I arrived at my destination. People were speaking Polish. I'd never been in such a foreign city as Chicago. Here there were new immigrants, *Nowa Emigracja.* The *Stara Polonia,* the older immigrants, had moved to the suburbs.

I wondered whether I'd find Stanislaus at the Orbis Restaurant on North Milwaukee Avenue, at the Podlasie Club, or at a school for English instruction run by an Iranian, *Pan* Manani. The school was in a vacant store. The men I watched were like Stanislaus when he'd come to our house. I observed two of them looking around beneath the first-floor window of a brick apartment building a block off North Milwaukee. When the window slid open, they handed in three packages from their coats. It was food, meat wrapped in butcher paper, maybe taken from a market down a block and across a parking lot. I watched a young girl in a white blouse, bright red jeans, and white plastic shoes carry things in a garbage bag while a man in a leather jacket and dark red pants yelled at her from across the street. The CTA bus honked at an old woman crossing in busy traffic. Carrying a bouquet of peonies upside down, she wore sandals. She had her nylons rolled like thick chains around her ankles.

No, no Stanislaus here, people told me. No Stanislaus anywhere. "Do you want to find him?" one couple asked. "Then maybe go to Polish Consulate on Lake Shore Drive."

I telephoned, asking whether they had information about a seaman who'd left a Polish freighter in Superior, Wisconsin, long ago.

They were accommodating. They were diplomatic. Mr. Sawicz, the vice-consul, said, "No news of such a sailor."

"If he has no money, if he has died, will you hear about it?" I asked.

"How could his body go to Poland, do you mean?"

"Yes, who would take Stanislaus home?"

"There is no money at consulate for this, but we can help to look for sponsors who will pay for his body to go back. One hundred and fifty bodies go each year of last three years. When Polish Airlines, LOT, was part of the State, when Poland was still communistic, LOT provided transportation. Now LOT is registered in court. It is company. No more communism. We can now only ask LOT for discount, that's all. The dead must have proper certificate of death with consulate stamp on it, have no communicable disease, be properly embalmed or cremated."

"But there's no word of the sailor Stanislaus Piotrowski?"

"No word. Can I help in another matter?" he asked.

I went back to the bus station wishing I could leave this earth forever.

Now far from shore where I have flown along caves of regret, I sing and draw the picture of the box of ancestry over and over, trace it, start drawing anew. HOW MANY WAYS DOES THE BOX OPEN?

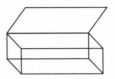

I whisper "love" and "truth," hear them, repeat them, hear Grażyna, hear ships, imagine a cockney bosun's mate, see *Dziaduś*'s part in history. I don't know where the seaman went when I was seventeen. How slight the sound the secrets of the past make. No one hears them. But there are such whispers circulating in a house.

Émigrés disappear like whispers. Haitians, Chinese, Mexicans came in 1987, came and vanished into the cities of America, into what books called "ethnic enclaves." Poles did, too. Many were here illegally, the *Nowa Emigracja*. You don't read about them much like you do about the others. No one cares about the Poles.

The sketches I make of the boxes he drew—I have them in this diary, the one I write in off and on. I keep the diary in the little drawer in my vanity. I want everything perfectly neat in the drawer in my room. If you hear the Polish words for "New Immigration"—"No-va Em-ee-gratza," Stanislaus would pronounce them—then this is what they mean. I am what they mean. I am a New Immigrant but so different from the Poles who came to America during that year, for the last page of hope is written out of my heart.

When I open the diary to my sketches, I hear a whisper: "HOW MANY WAYS CAN THE BOX OPEN, CATHERINE?"

I find four ways, no, four thousand or more. The best thing was for me to tell the story in writing. *You* look at this story. I wrote it on nights when I had a light blue shade on the lamp in my room, on nights of heavy seas and lightning. I turned up the light on the vanity, prayed to the Black Madonna of Częstochowa, and wrote these pages. If anyone asked why, I'd tell them, "I wrote them for love," though they might not believe that this could happen in the East End of Superior, Wisconsin.

—Signed: Catherine Kalinowski

ANTHONY BUKOSKI is the author of four other story collections, including *Children of Strangers* (SMU, 1993), *Polonaise* (SMU, 1999), and *Time Between Trains* (SMU, 2003), which was a *Booklist* Editors' Choice. His stories have been featured on Wisconsin Public Radio, National Public Radio, and in live performance in the "Selected Shorts" series at Symphony Space in New York City. He teaches at his alma mater, the University of Wisconsin in his hometown of Superior, where his Polish émigré grandparents settled early in the last century.